OTHER BOOKS BY JEFF KINNEY

Diary of a Wimpy Kid

Diary of a Wimpy Kid: Rodrick Rules

Diary of a Wimpy Kid: The Last Straw

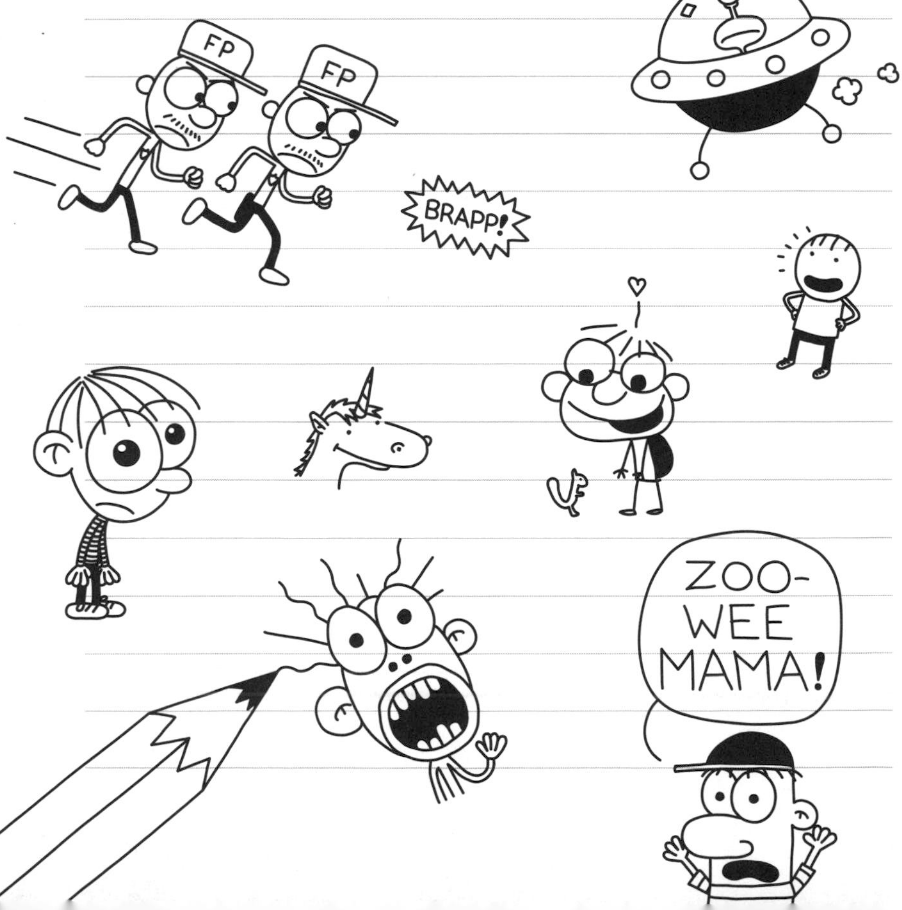
FP
FP
BRAPP!
ZOO-WEE MAMA!

DIARY
of a Wimpy Kid
Do-It-Yourself
Book

by Jeff Kinney

YOUR
PICTURE
HERE

AMULET BOOKS

New York

PUBLISHER'S NOTE: This is a work of fiction. Names, characters, places, and incidents are either the product of the author's imagination or are used fictitiously, and any resemblance to actual persons, living or dead, business establishments, events, or locales is entirely coincidental.

Library of Congress Control Number: 2008927175

ISBN 978-0-8109-7977-2

Book design by Jeff Kinney
Cover design by Chad W. Beckerman and Jeff Kinney

Published in 2008 by Amulet Books, an imprint of Harry N. Abrams, Inc.

Printed and bound in U.S.A.
16 15 14 13 12 11 10 9

HNA
harry n. abrams, inc.
a subsidiary of La Martinière Groupe
115 West 18th Street
New York, NY 10011
www.hnabooks.com

THIS BOOK BELONGS TO:

Tyler Ferry

IF FOUND, PLEASE RETURN
TO THIS ADDRESS:

700 riverwood LN iN
The Neighborhood of willow oak

(NO REWARD)

What're you gonna do with this thing?

OK, this is your book now, so technically you can do whatever you want with it.

BONK
HEY!

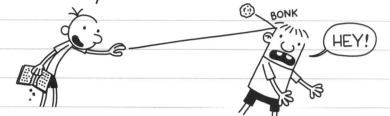

But if you write anything in this journal, make sure you hold on to it. Because one day you're gonna want to show people what you were like back when you were a kid.

WOW, HE WAS INCREDIBLY SMART AND WITTY EVEN THEN!
IT'S TRUE!

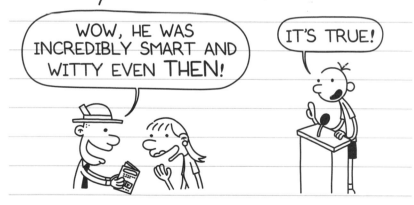

Whatever you do, just make sure you don't write down your "feelings" in here. Because one thing's for sure: This is NOT a diary.

Your DESERT

If you were gonna be marooned for the rest of your life, what would you want to have with you?

Video games
1. Ben ten
2. ~~I'm fat~~ super smash bros, mella
3. ~~eat it~~ family guy

Songs
1. god bless the U.S.A.
2. ~~family guy~~ Ben ten
3. ~~family guy~~ eat it

ISI AND piⁿks

Books

1. twilight
2. Diray of a wimpy Kid 1
3. Diray of a wimpy Kid 4

Movies

1. Fantastic Four
2. Charle and the choclate factory
3. speed racer

Have you

Have you ever gotten a haircut that was so bad you needed to stay home from school?

YES ☐ NO ☑

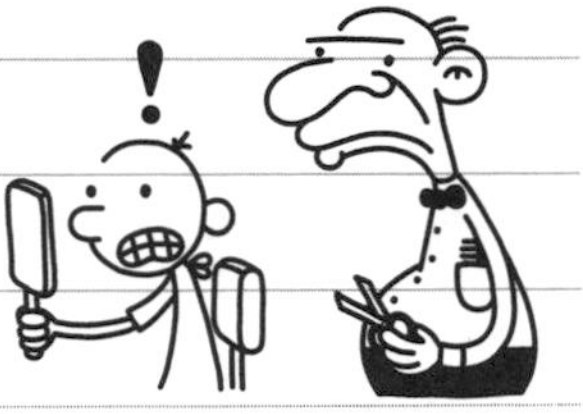

Have you ever had to put suntan lotion on a grown-up?

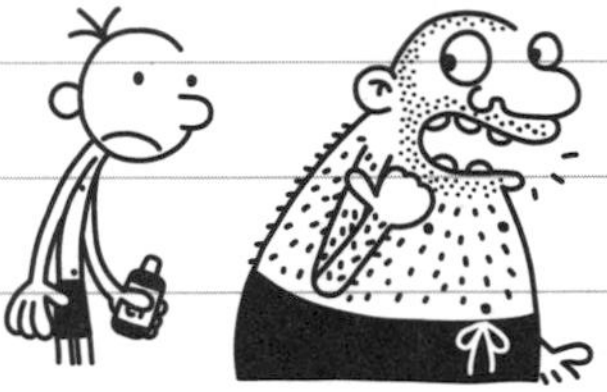

YES ☑ NO ☐

Have you ever been bitten by an animal?

YES ☐
NO ☑

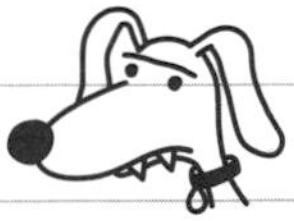

Have you ever been bitten by a person?

YES ☑
NO ☐

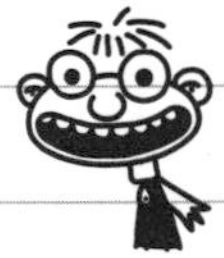

Have you ever tried to blow a bubble with a mouthful of raisins?

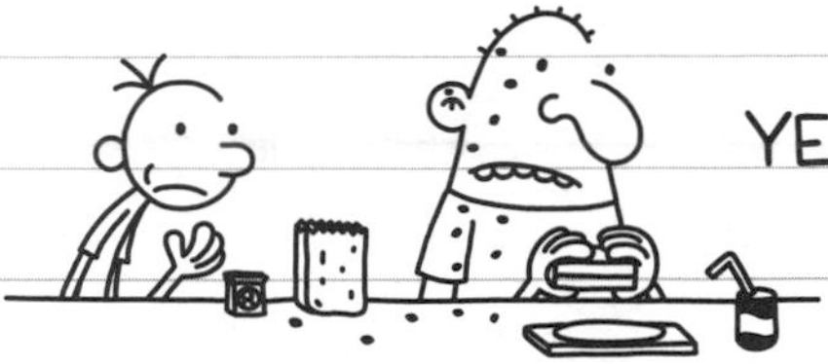

YES ☐ NO ☑

EVER...

Have you ever peed in a swimming pool?

YES ☑ NO ☐

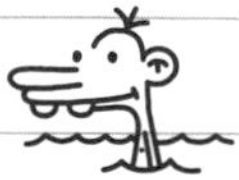

Have you ever been kissed full on the lips by a relative who's older than seventy?

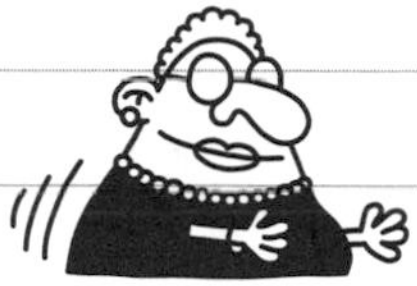

YES ☒ NO ☑

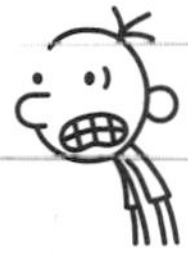

Have you ever been sent home early by one of your friends' parents?

YES ☐ NO ☑

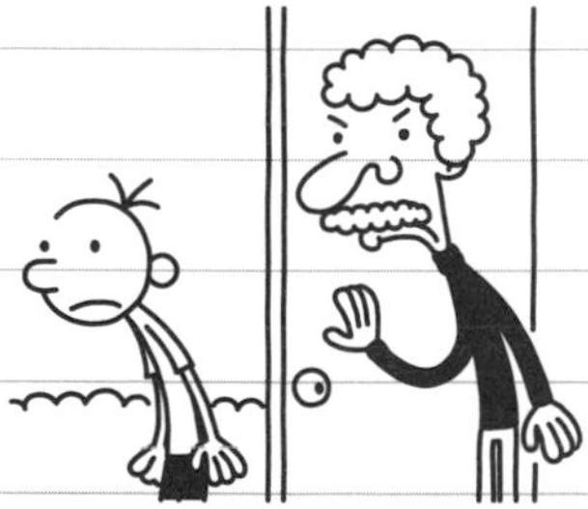

Have you ever had to change a diaper?

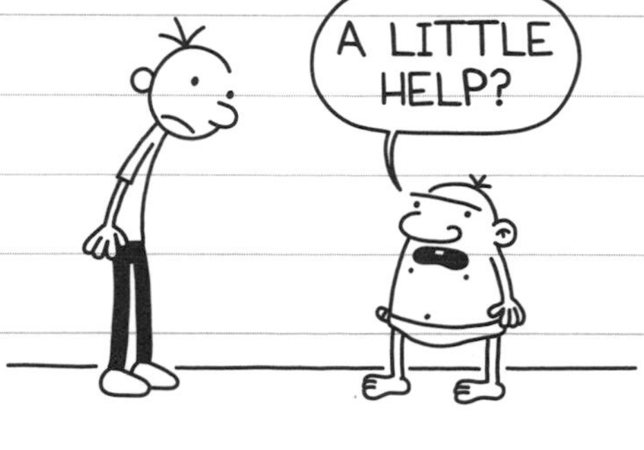
A LITTLE HELP?

YES ☐ NO ☑

PERSONALITY

What's your favorite ANIMAL?

snake

Write down FOUR ADJECTIVES that describe why you like that animal:

(EXAMPLE: FRIENDLY, COOL, ETC.)

cool   Slithery

awesome   unfriendly

What's your favorite COLOR?

Neon   green

Write down FOUR ADJECTIVES that describe why you like that color:

cool   Bright

awesome   Very green

The adjectives you wrote down for your favorite ANIMAL
describe HOW YOU THINK OF YOURSELF.
The adjectives you wrote down for your favorite COLOR
describe HOW OTHER PEOPLE THINK OF YOU.

TEST

ANSWER THESE QUESTIONS AND THEN FLIP THE BOOK UPSIDE DOWN TO FIND OUT THINGS YOU NEVER KNEW ABOUT YOURSELF.

What's the title of the last BOOK you read?

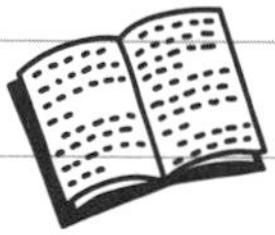

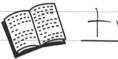

twilight

List FOUR ADJECTIVES that describe what you thought of that book:

cool — a little nice

awesome — they were unfriendly

What's the name of your favorite MOVIE?

Hotel for dogs

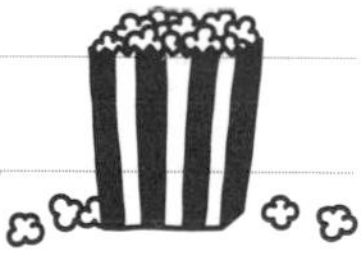

Write down FOUR ADJECTIVES that describe why you liked that movie:

Cool — frendliy

awsome — Funny

The adjectives you wrote down for the last BOOK you read describe HOW YOU THINK OF SCHOOL.

The adjectives you wrote down for your favorite MOVIE describe WHAT YOU'LL BE LIKE in thirty years.

Unfinished

Zoo-Wee Mama!

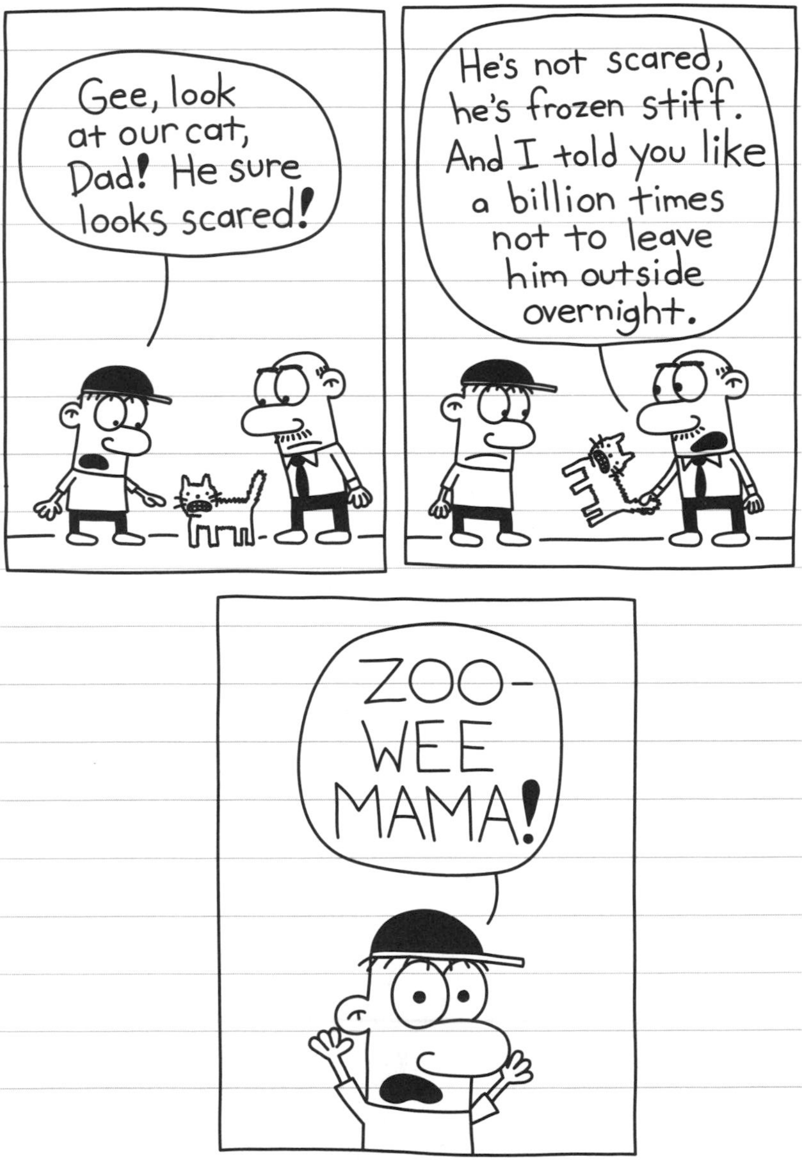
Gee, look at our cat, Dad! He sure looks scared!
He's not scared, he's frozen stiff. And I told you like a billion times not to leave him outside overnight.
ZOO-WEE MAMA!

COMICS

Zoo-Wee Mama!

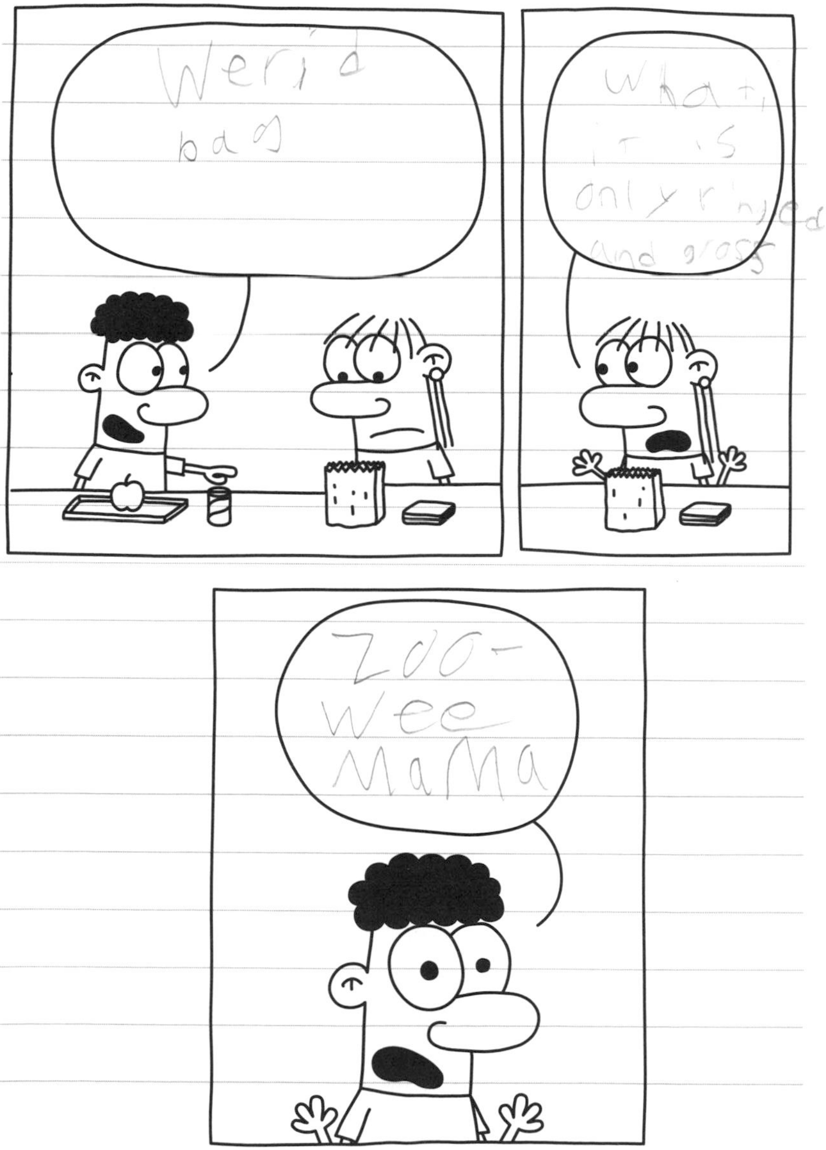
Werid bag
Zoo-wee Mama

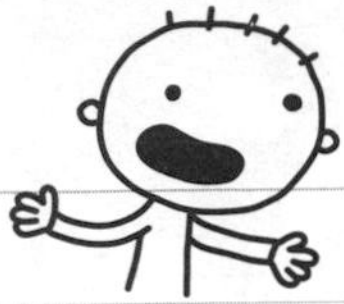

Make your

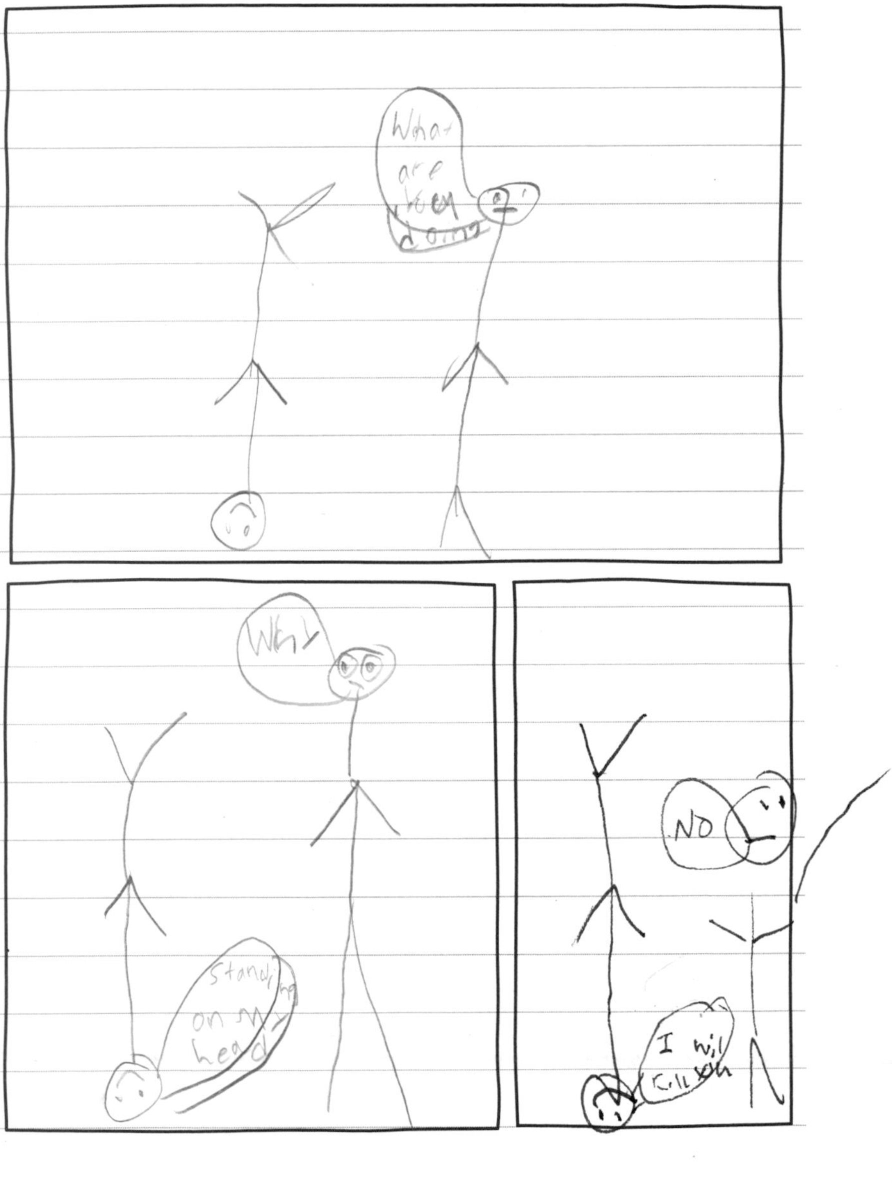
What are
Why
Standing on my head
NO
I wil

OWN comics

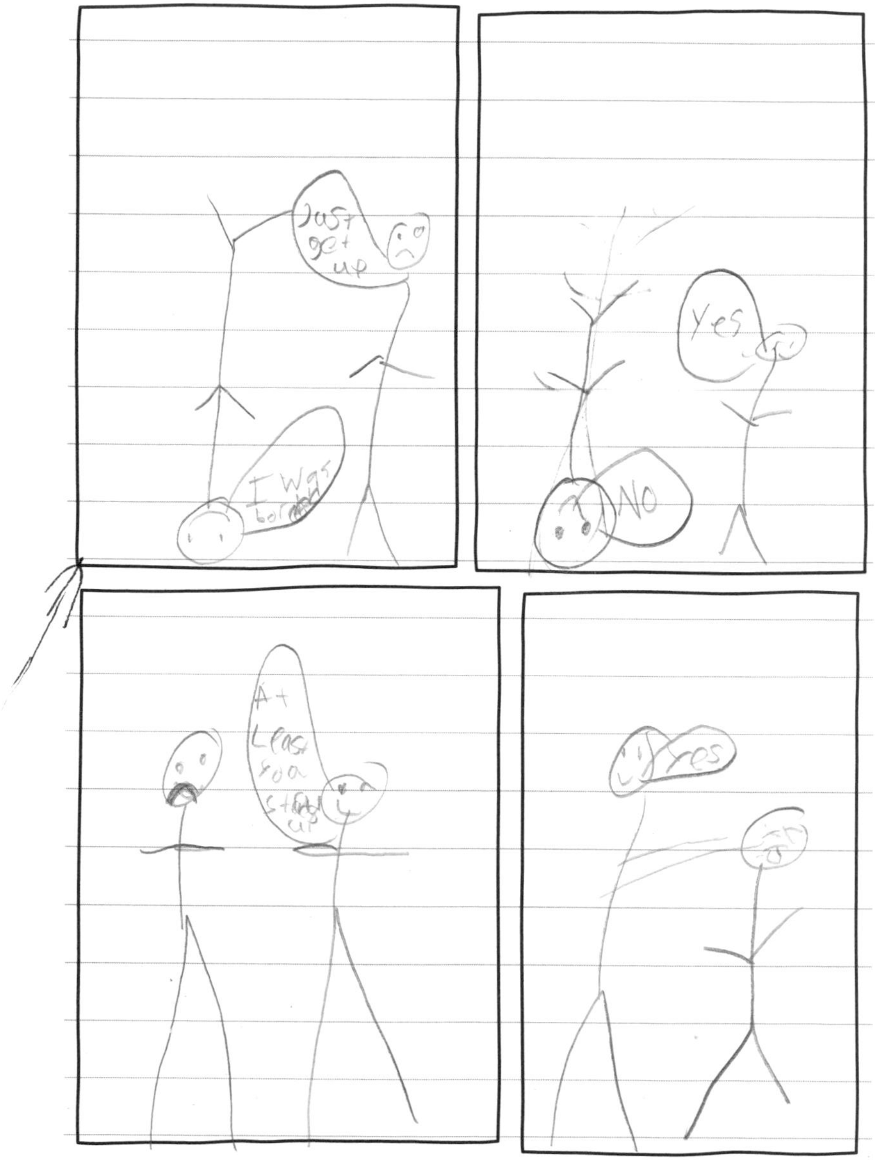
Just get up
I was
Yes
No
At Least
Yes

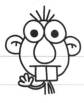

Predict the

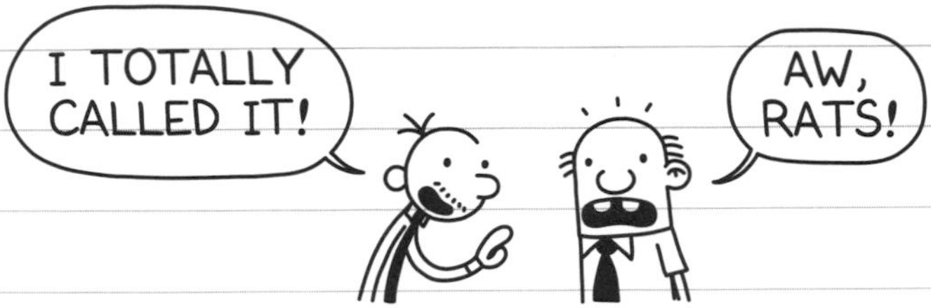
I TOTALLY CALLED IT!
AW, RATS!

I officially predict that twenty years from now cars will run on ___Energt___ instead of gasoline. A cheeseburger will cost $___1___, and a ticket to the movies will cost $___2___. Pets will have their own ___Bed___s. Underwear will be made out of ___Skin___. ___polor bears___ will no longer exist. A ___Cat___ named ___Super Cat___ will be president. There will be more ___Wbugs___ than people.

The annoying catchphrase will be:

Cooly word, My Aooly

No biggie

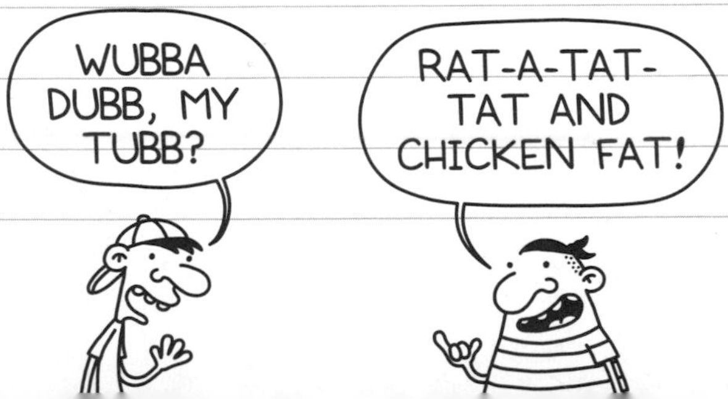
WUBBA DUBB, MY TUBB?
RAT-A-TAT-TAT AND CHICKEN FAT!

FUTURE

Aliens will visit our planet in the year 2999 and make the following announcement:

I will tell ya
all things
You weren't suppost to eat

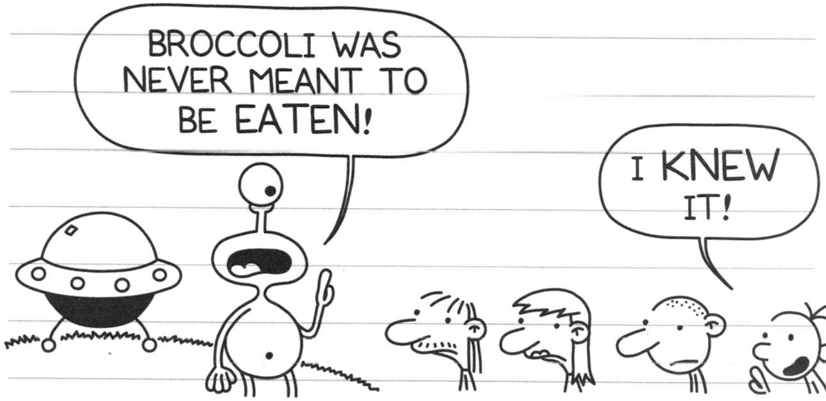
BROCCOLI WAS NEVER MEANT TO BE EATEN!
I KNEW IT!

The number-one thing that will get on old people's nerves twenty years from now will be:

tolit paper his
houes

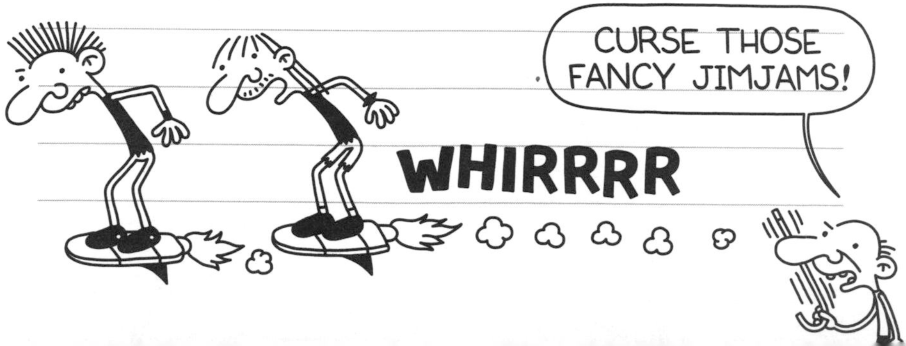
CURSE THOSE FANCY JIMJAMS!
WHIRRRR

Predict the

IN FIFTY YEARS:

Robots and mankind will be locked in a battle for supremacy. TRUE ☑ FALSE ☐

HA!
DOINK
HEY! QUIT IT!

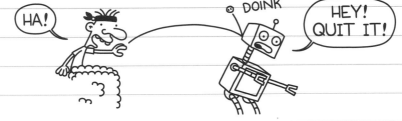

Parents will be banned from dancing within twenty feet of their children. TRUE ☐ FALSE ☑

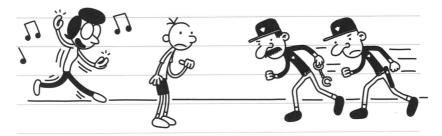

People will have instant-messaging chips implanted in their brains. TRUE ☐ FALSE ☑

u r a dork
:(

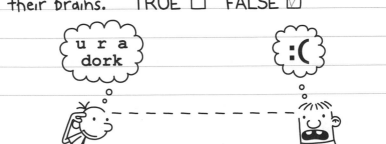

FUTURE

YOUR FIVE BOLD PREDICTIONS FOR THE FUTURE:

1. There will be flying cars

2. You can fly in the furrae

3. there will be robots

4. You can reed people's mind

5. There will be fairies

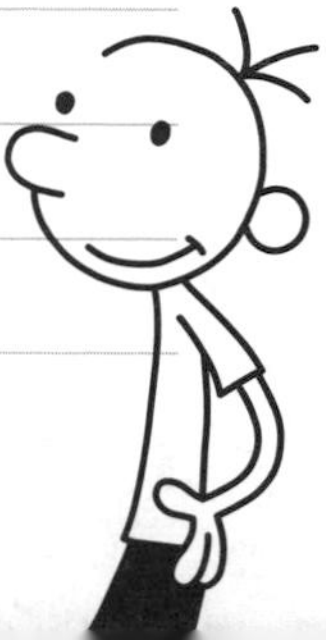

(WRITE EVERYTHING DOWN NOW SO YOU CAN TELL YOUR FRIENDS "I TOLD YOU SO" LATER ON.)

Predict YOUR

What you're basically gonna do here is roll a die over and over, crossing off items when you land on them, like this:

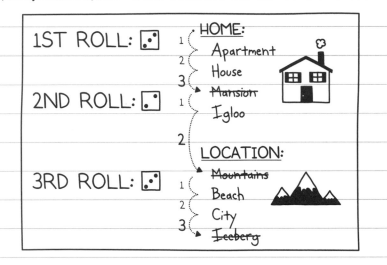

1ST ROLL: ⚁

2ND ROLL: ⚁

3RD ROLL: ⚂

1
2
3

HOME:
Apartment
House
~~Mansion~~
Igloo

1
2

LOCATION:
~~Mountains~~
Beach
City
~~Iceberg~~

1
2
3

Keep going through the list, and when you get to the end, jump back to the beginning. When there's only one item left in a category, circle it. Once you've got an item in each category circled, you'll know your future! Good luck!

MY LIFE STINKS.

future

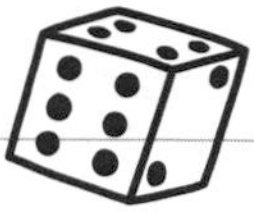
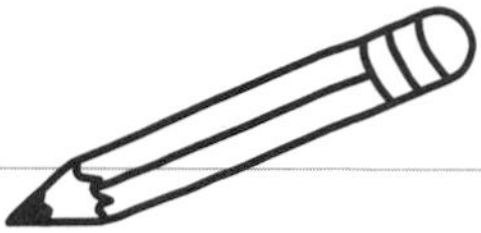

HOME:

Apartment

House

~~Mansion~~

Igloo

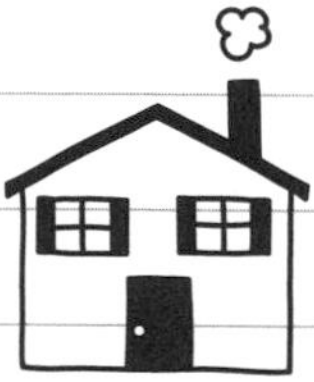

LOCATION:

Mountains

Beach

~~City~~

Iceberg

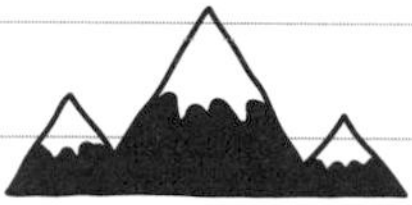

JOB:

Doctor

Actor

Clown

Mechanic

Lawyer

Pilot

Pro athlete

Dentist

Magician

~~Whatever you want~~

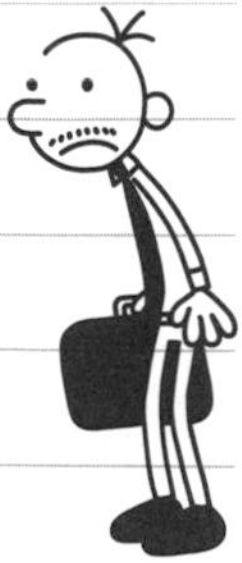

KIDS:

None

One

~~Two~~

Ten

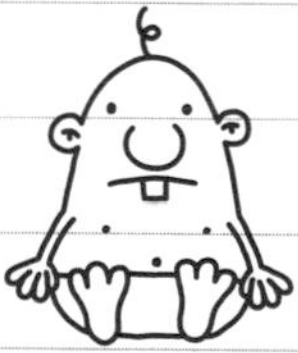

VEHICLE:

Car

Motorcycle

~~Helicopter~~

Skateboard

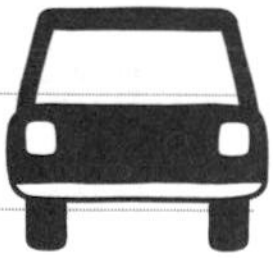

PET:

Dog

Cat

Bird

~~Turtle~~

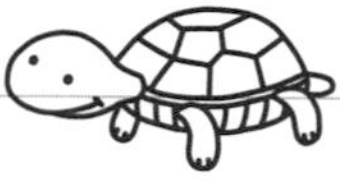

SALARY:

$100 a year

$100,000 a year

$1 million a year

~~$100 million a year~~

Design your

GREG HEFFLEY'S FUTURE HOUSE

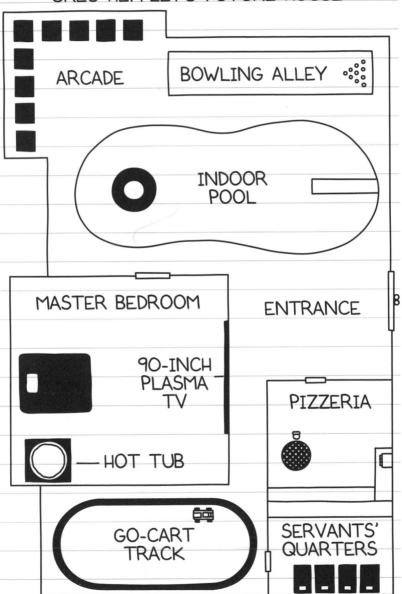

ARCADE

BOWLING ALLEY

INDOOR POOL

MASTER BEDROOM

ENTRANCE

90-INCH PLASMA TV

— HOT TUB

PIZZERIA

GO-CART TRACK

SERVANTS' QUARTERS

DREAM HOUSE

YOUR FUTURE HOUSE

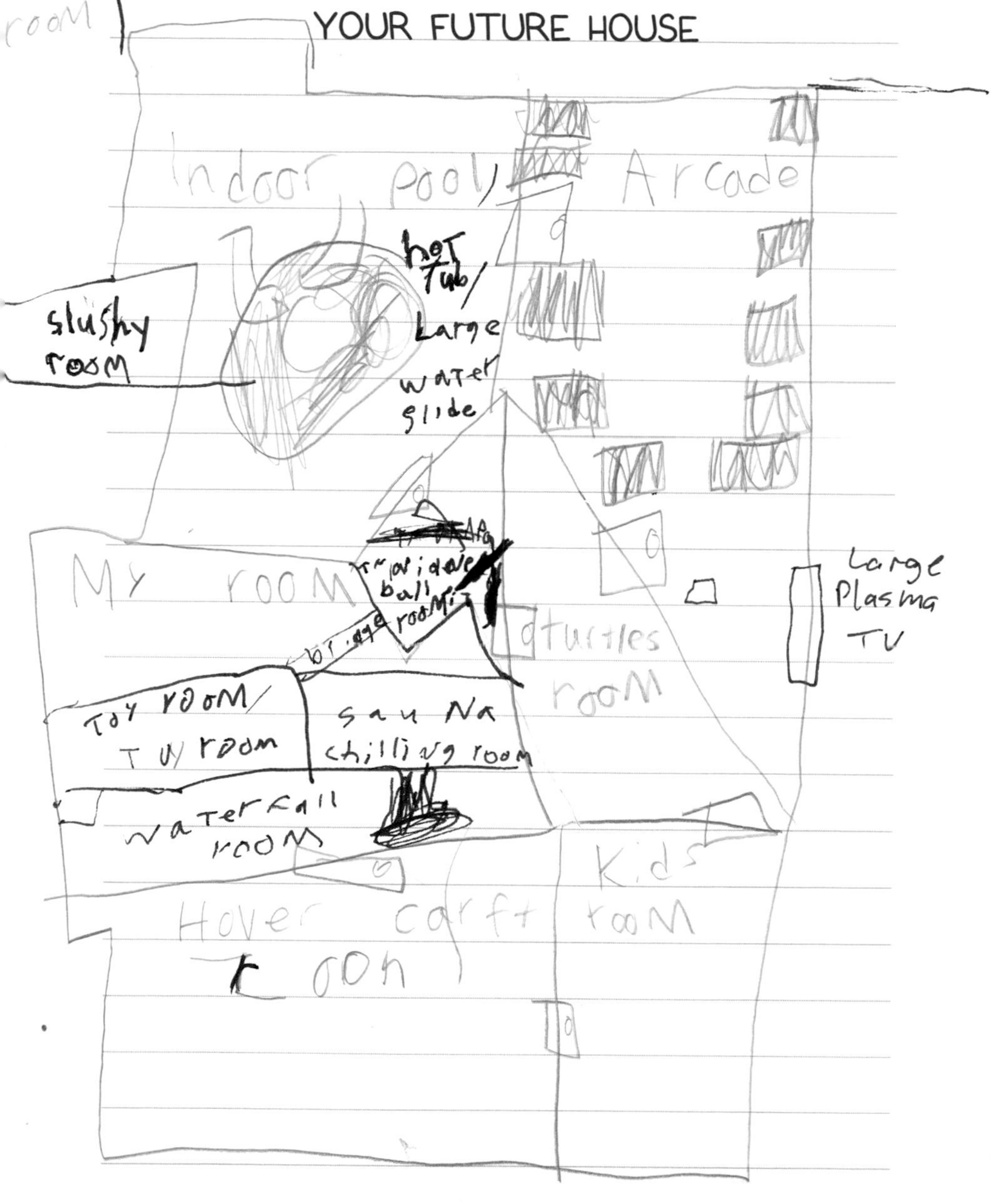

roller coser room
Indoor pool
Arcade
hot tub/ Large water glide
slushy room
My room
bridge ball room
bridge
turtles room
Large Plasma TV
Toy room/ TV room
sauna chilling room
waterfall room
Kids room
Hover carft room

A few questions

What's the most embarrassing thing that ever happened to someone who wasn't you?

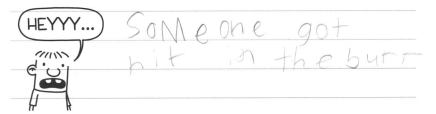

SoMeone got hit in the burr

What's the worst thing you ever ate?

badMiytSalad, aNd faxe salt

How many steps does it take you to jump into bed after you turn off the light?

4 Steps

How much would you be willing to pay for an extra hour of sleep in the morning?

1 dollor

from GREG

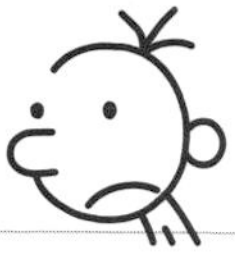

Have you ever pretended you were sick so you could stay home from school?

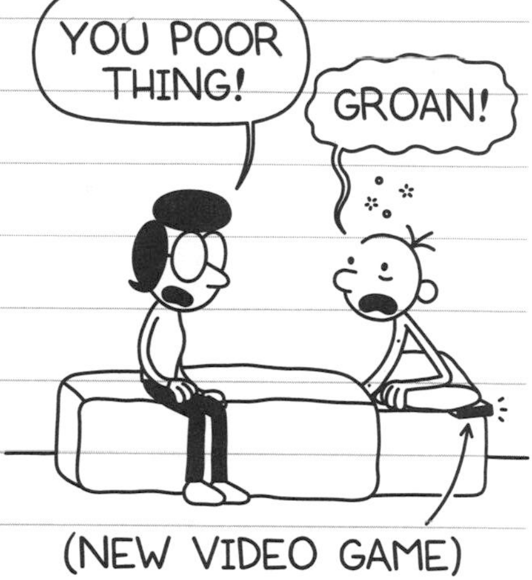
YOU POOR THING!
GROAN!
(NEW VIDEO GAME)

NO

Does it get on your nerves when people skip?

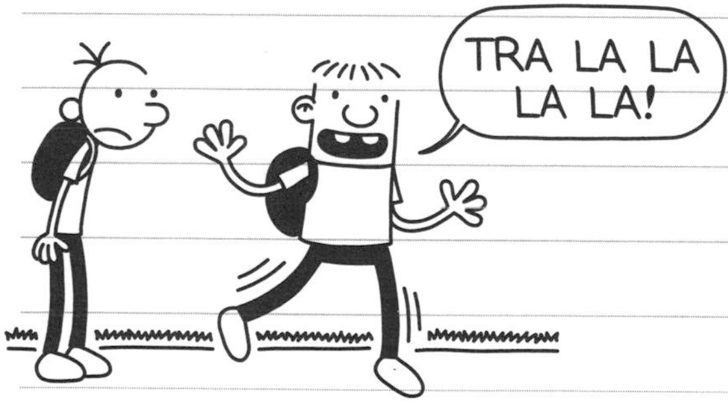
TRA LA LA LA LA!

Yes and No

Did you ever do something bad that you never got busted for? yes

Unfinished

Ugly Eugene

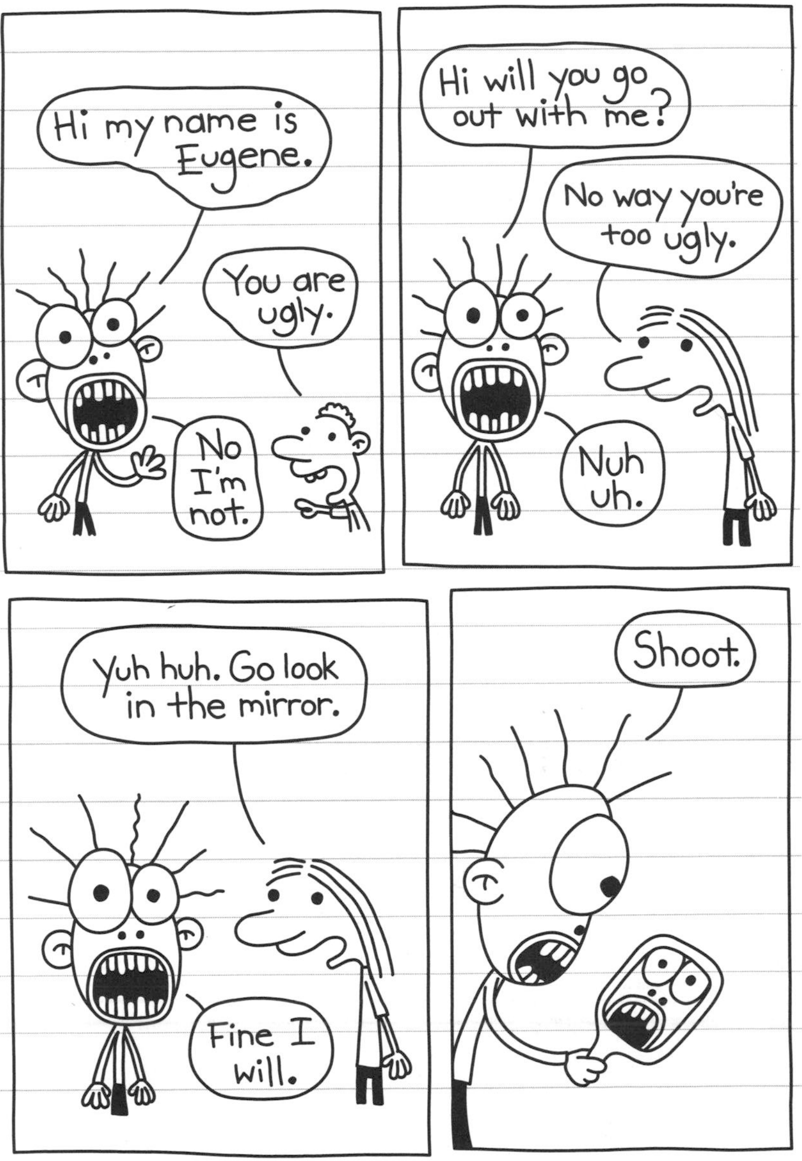
Hi my name is Eugene.
You are ugly.
No I'm not.
Hi will you go out with me?
No way you're too ugly.
Nuh uh.
Yuh huh. Go look in the mirror.
Fine I will.
Shoot.

COMICS

Ugly Eugene

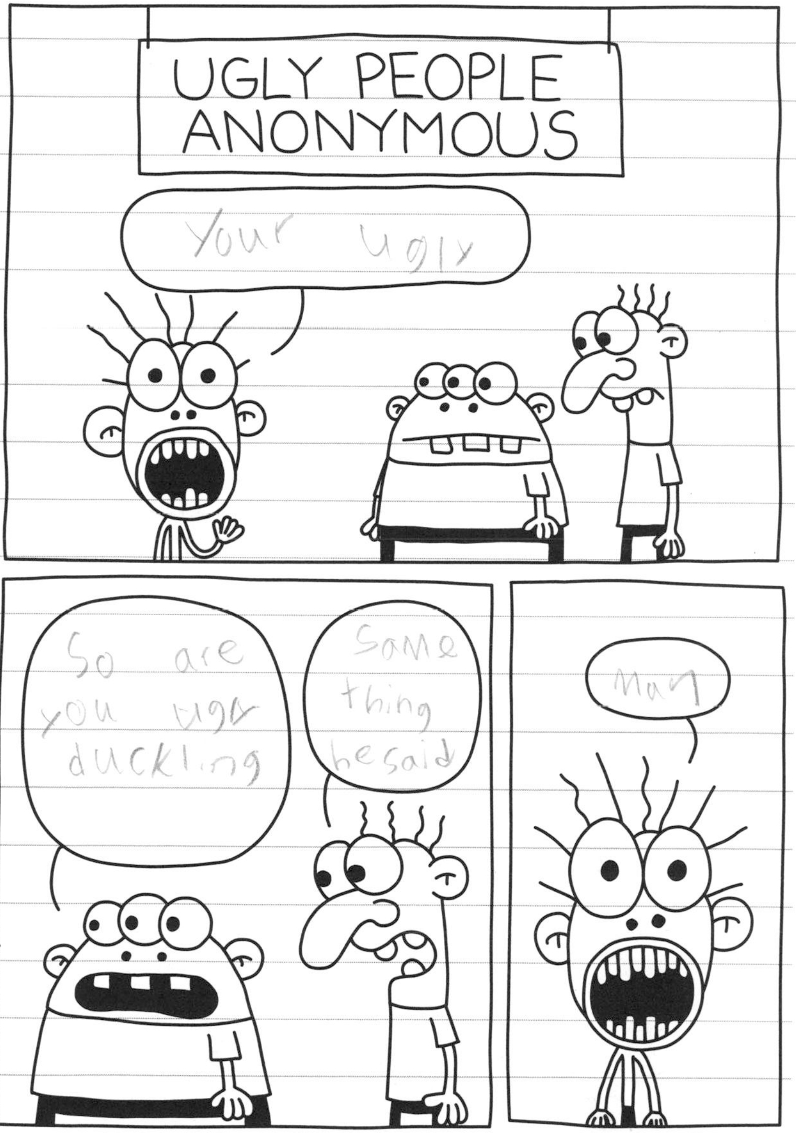
UGLY PEOPLE ANONYMOUS
Your ugly
So are you ugly duckling
Same thing he said
Man

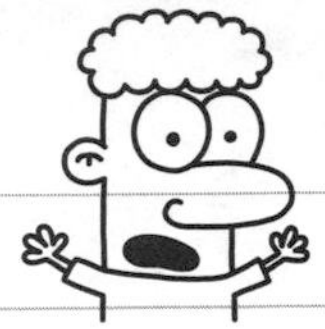

Make your

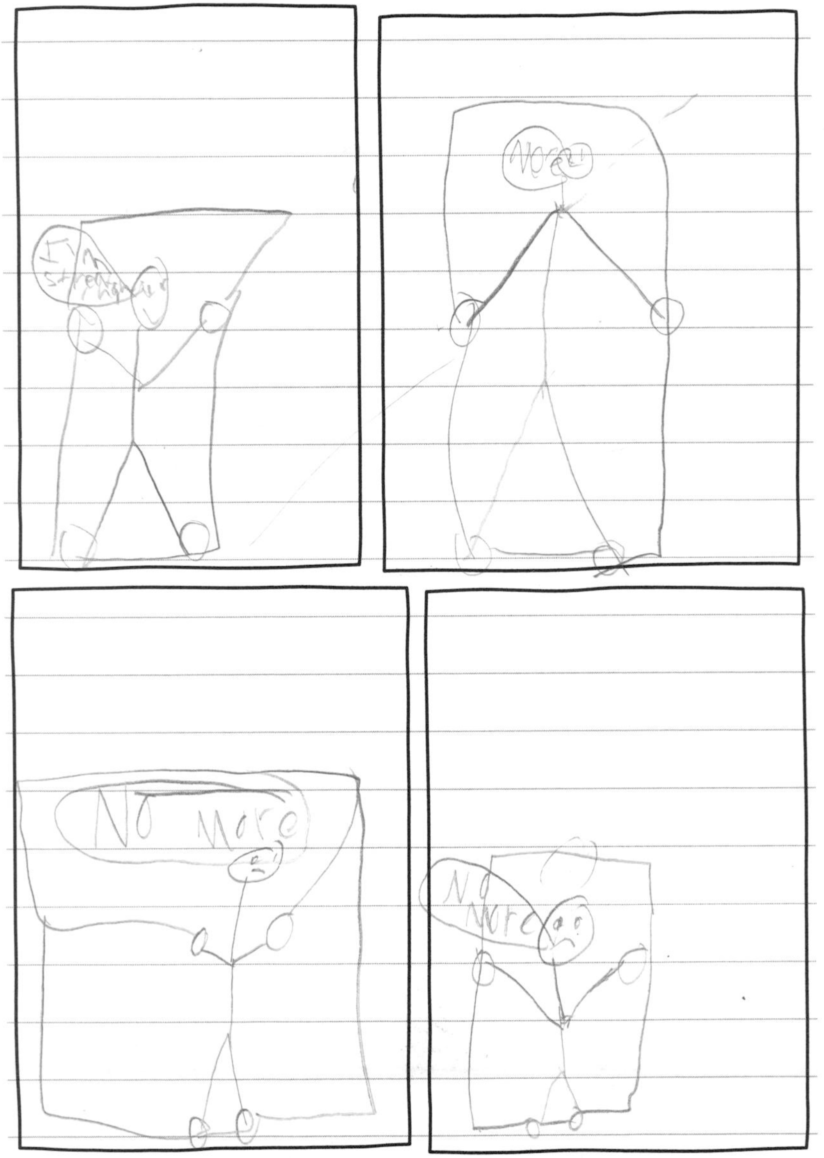
No more
No more

OWN comics

More
Too Much
Much
You think

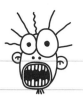

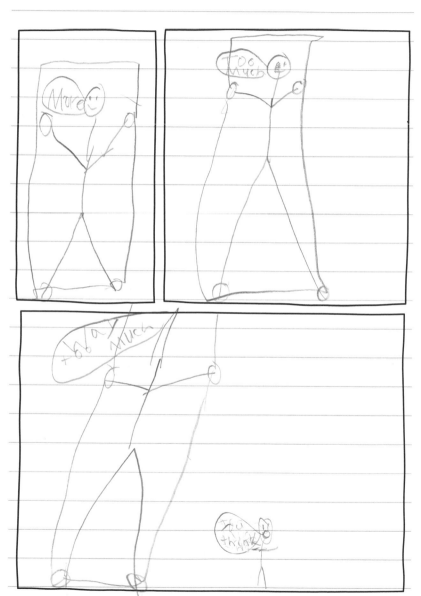

Good advice for

1. Don't use the bathroom on the second floor, because there aren't any stall doors in there.

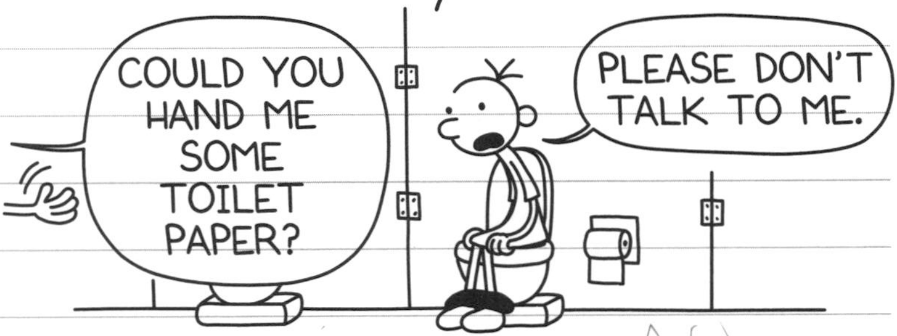
COULD YOU HAND ME SOME TOILET PAPER?
PLEASE DON'T TALK TO ME.

2. Be careful who you sit next to in the cafeteria.

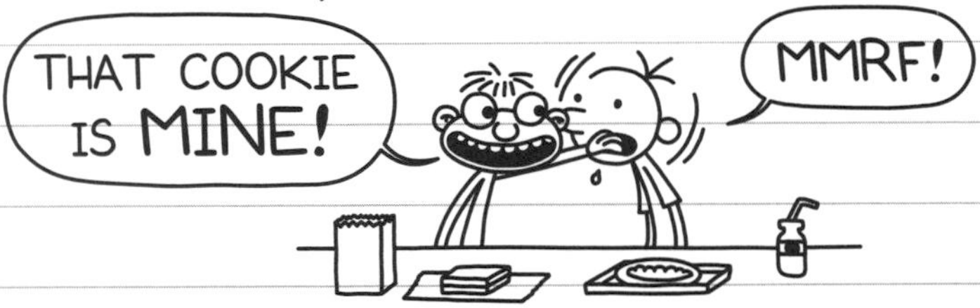
THAT COOKIE IS MINE!
MMRF!

3. Don't pick your nose right before you get your school picture taken.

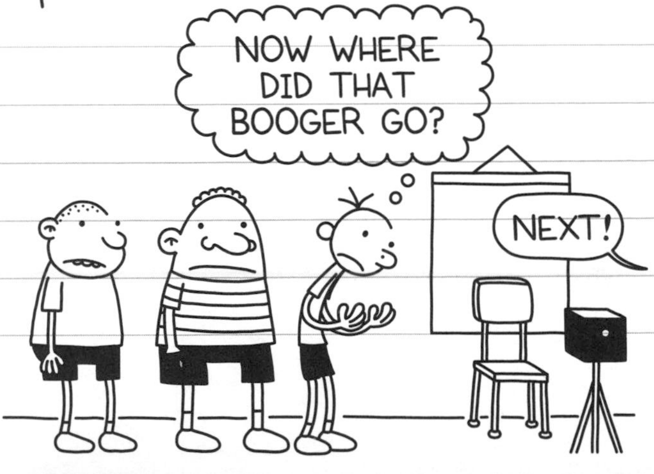
NOW WHERE DID THAT BOOGER GO?
NEXT!

next year's class

1. Smarter

2. cooler

3. funnyer

4. Nicer

Draw your FAMILY

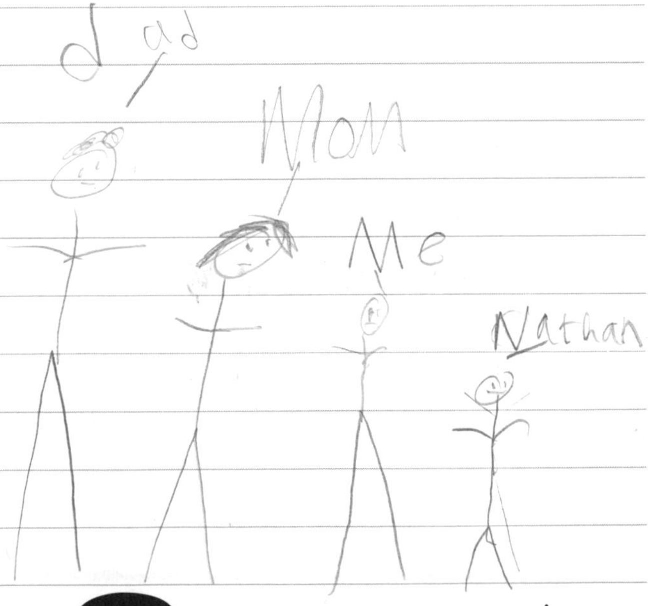
dad
Mom
Me
Nathan

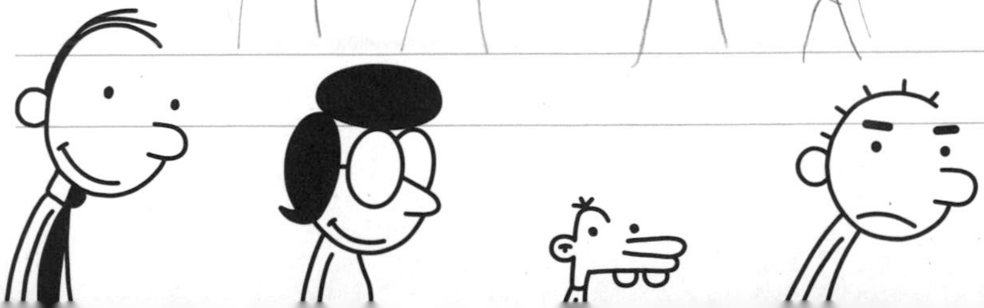

the way Greg Heffley would

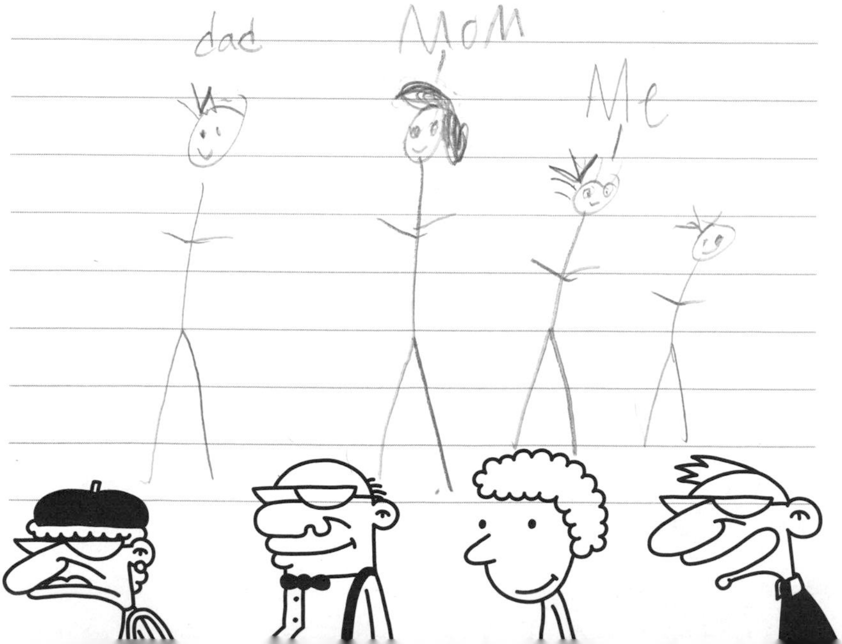
dad
Mom
Me

Your FAVORITES

TV show: Witsholag
Band: Joans brothers
Sports team: pathers
Food: Pizza
Celebrity: TONY Hawk
Smell: Pizza
Villain: VenoM
Shoe brand: air aters
Store: Joesoph beth
Soda: PiNK LemoNude
Cereal: cinnomn toast
Super hero: SPider Man
Candy: baby bottle pop
Restaurant: out back
Athlete: Michal Jordan
Game system: Wii
Comic strip: Spider Man
Magazine: Store items
Car: Limo

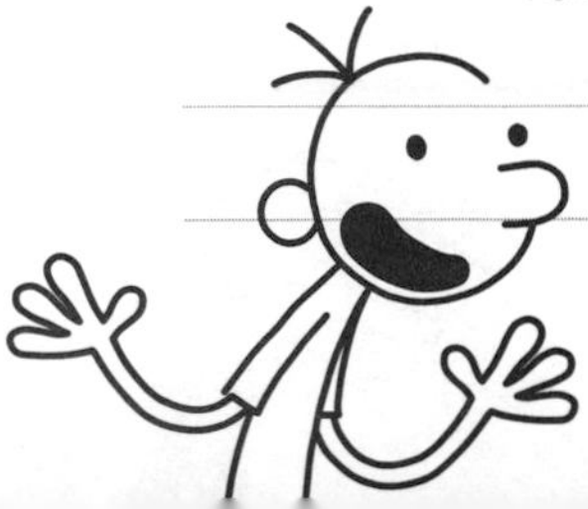

Your LEAST favorites

TV show: Star Wars
Band: Beethoven
Sports team: Lovilla
Food: Brusle sprots
Celebrity: Beethoven
Smell: Lice repellent
Villain: darth vader
Shoe brand: tieing Shoes
Store: clotheing store
Soda: Ornage ade
Cereal: School
Super hero: Timber thunder
Candy: Suger free Lollx Pop
Restaurant: chills
Athlete: David Becom
Game system: game box
Comic strip: Star Wars
Magazine: WoMans
Car: bug

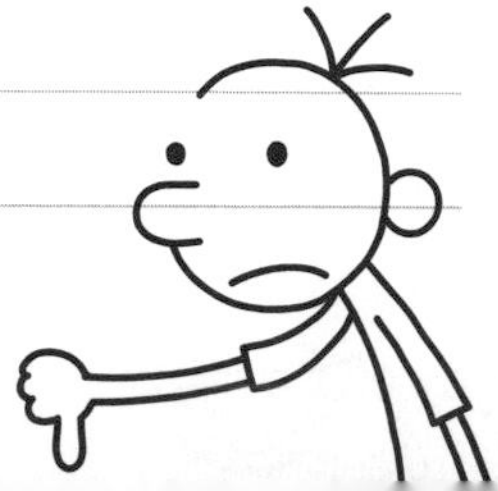

Things you should do
I did These Things

- ☑ Stay up all night.
- ☑ Ride on a roller coaster with a loop in it.
- ☑ Get in a food fight. 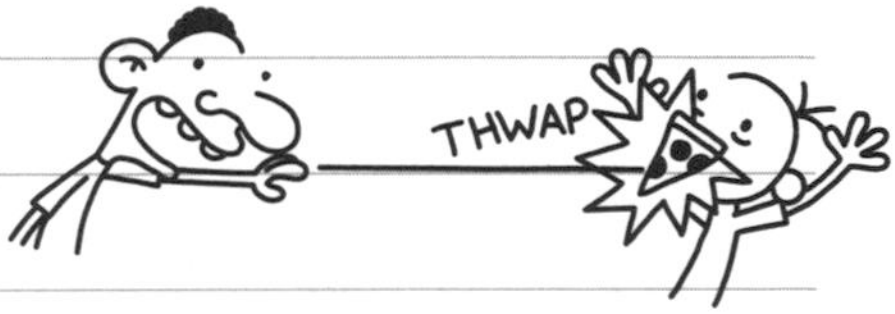 THWAP
- ☐ Get an autograph from a famous person.
- ☑ Get a hole in one in miniature golf. 
- ☐ Give yourself a haircut.
- ☑ Write down an idea for an invention.
- ☑ Spend three nights in a row away from home.
- ☑ Mail someone a letter with a real stamp and everything.

Dear Gramma, Please send money.

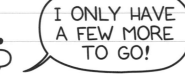

I ONLY HAVE A FEW MORE TO GO!

before you ~~get~~ old

I get

- [x] Go on a campout.

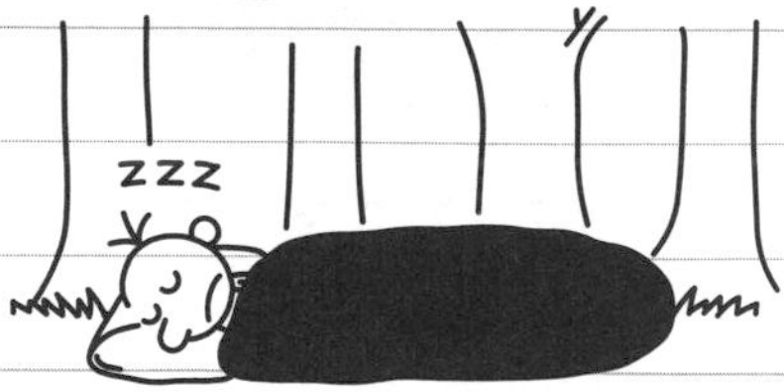
ZZZ

- [x] Read a whole book with no pictures in it.

- [x] Beat someone who's older than you in a footrace.

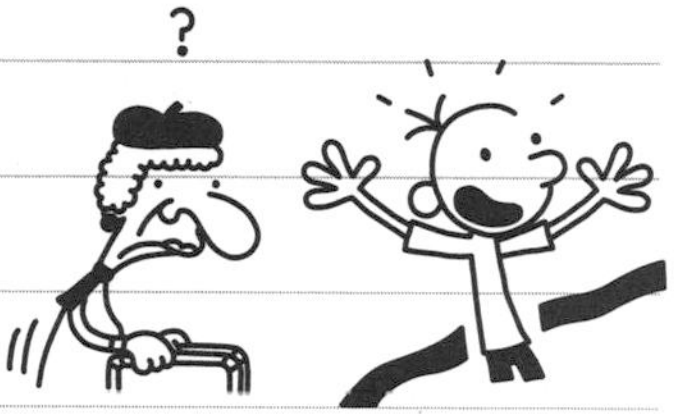
?

- [x] Make it through a whole lollipop without biting it.

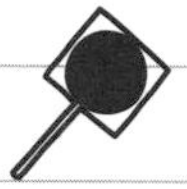

- [x] Use a porta-potty.

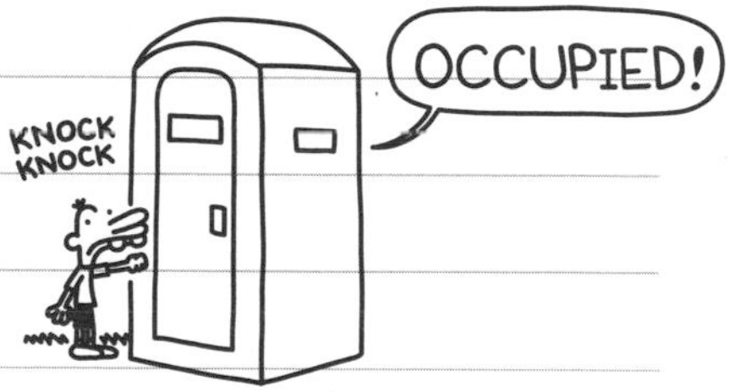
KNOCK KNOCK
OCCUPIED!

- [x] Score at least one point in an organized sport.

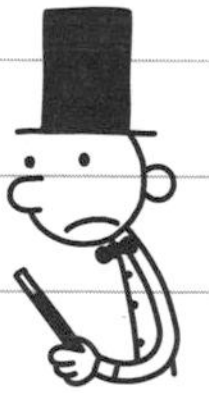

- [ ] Try out for a talent show.

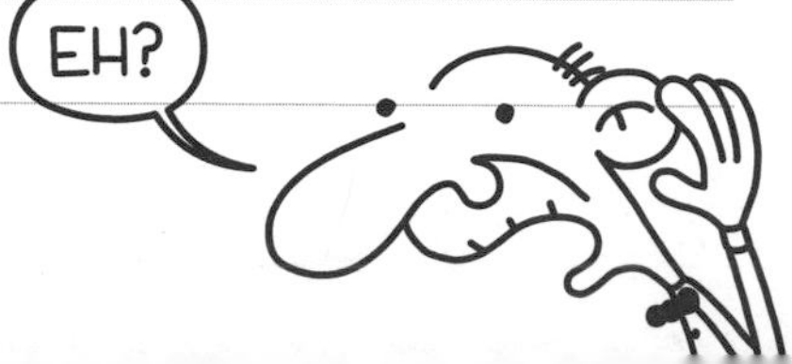
EH?

Five things NOBODY KNOWS about you

BECAUSE THEY NEVER BOTHERED TO ASK

1. I Make a Werid hosjes

2. I Like chess

3. I Love Webkinz

4. I Love cLub penguiN

5. I Make easy Frends

I CAN PUT MY WHOLE FOOT IN MY MOUTH!

YOU'RE GROSS!

The WORST NIGHTMARE you ever had

I was geting
Killed by a very
very very very
bad villan

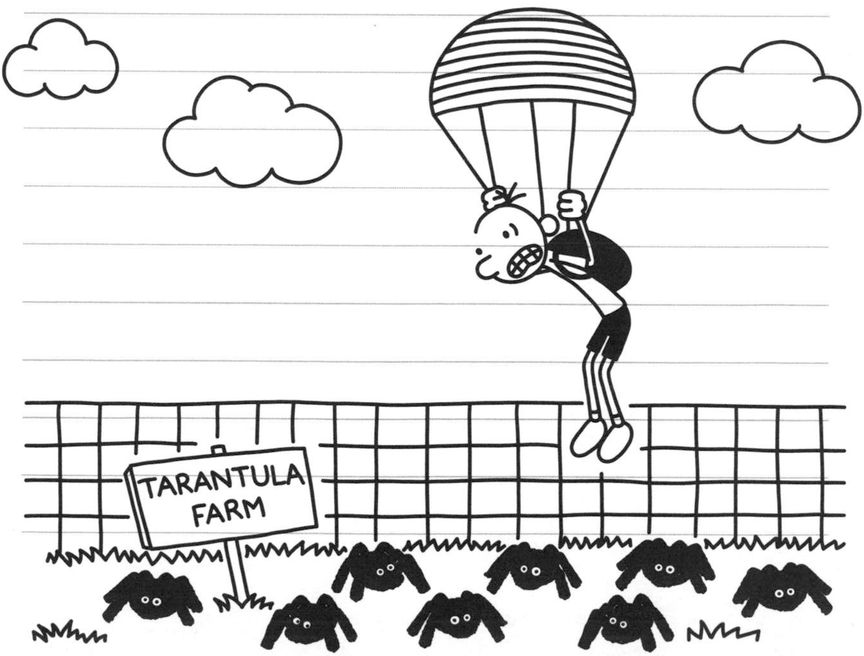
TARANTULA
FARM

Rules for your

1. Don't talk to me before 8:00 in the morning.

2. Don't make me sit next to my little brother on spaghetti night.

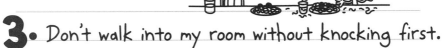

3. Don't walk into my room without knocking first.

4. Don't borrow my underwear under any circumstances.

FAMILY

1. No curseing

2. No ball in the houes

3. No back talking

4. No sliding down the staris

Your life, by

Longest you've ever gone without bathing:

4 Months

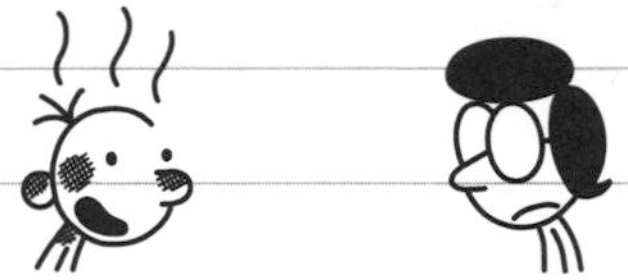

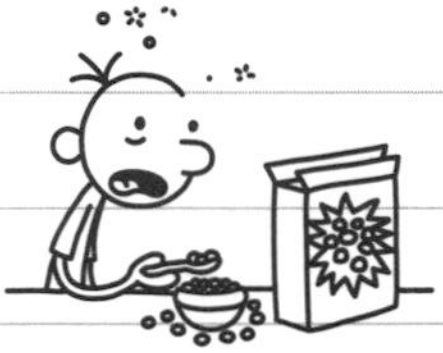

Most bowls of cereal you've ever eaten at one time:

2

Longest you've ever been grounded: 0 Seconds

Latest you've ever been for school:

0 Seconds

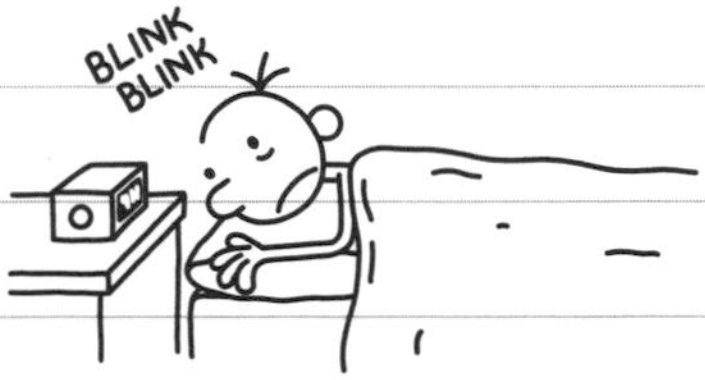
BLINK
BLINK

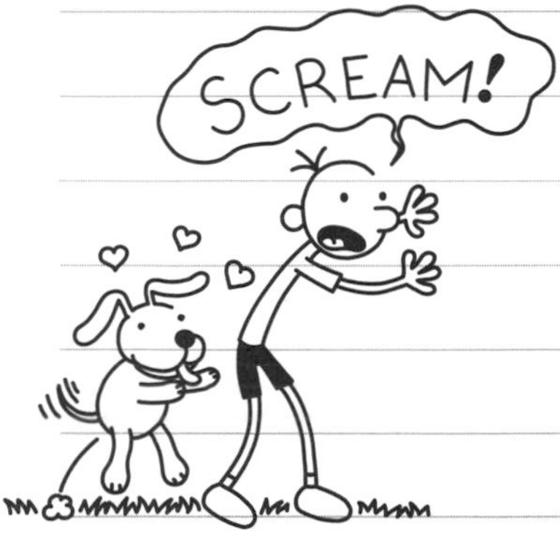
SCREAM!

Number of times you've been chased by a dog:

10

Number of times you've been locked out of the house:

3

the numbers

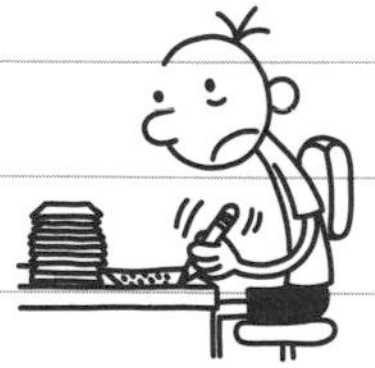

Most hours you've spent doing homework in one night:

7

Most money you've ever saved up: $70.99

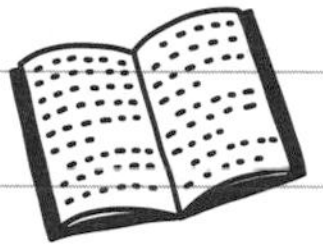

Length of the shortest book you've ever used for a book report:

20 pages

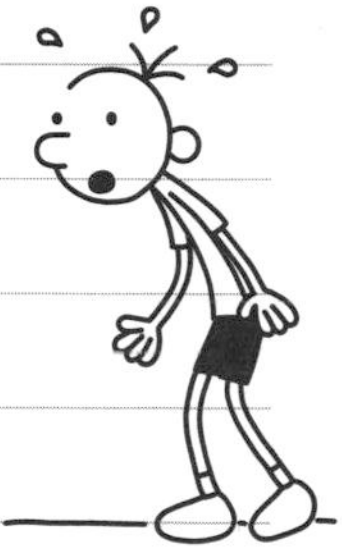

Farthest distance you've ever walked:

8 Miles

Longest you've ever gone without watching TV:

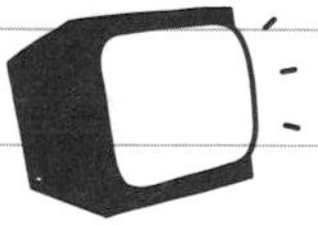

7 days

Number of times you've gotten caught picking your nose:

21

Number of times you've gotten away with picking your nose:

7,487

Unfinished

Li'l Cutie

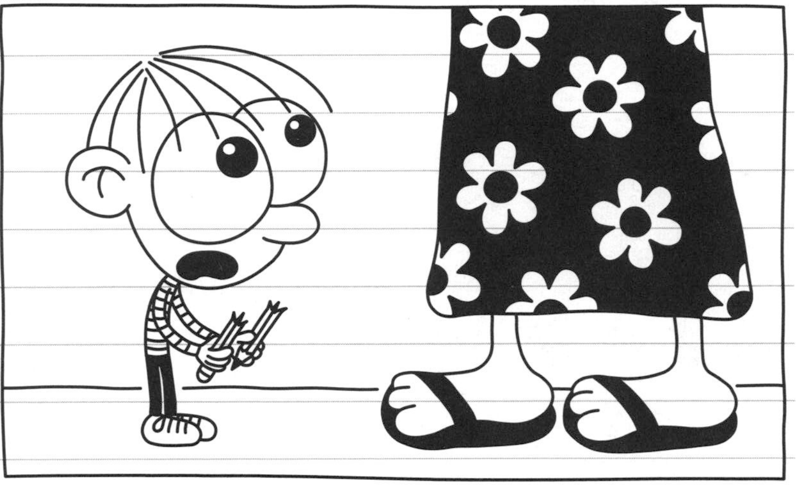

" *Mommy, did my pencil go to heaven?* "

Li'l Cutie

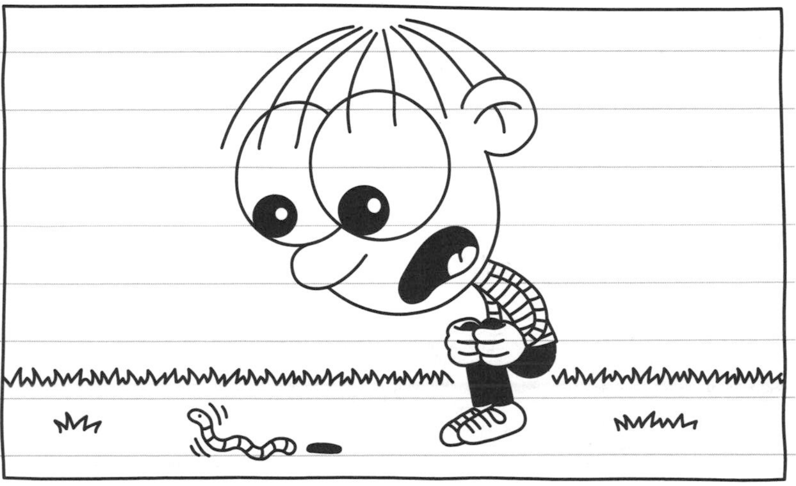

" I think worms dont "

COMICS

Li'l Cutie

" I didn't do it "

Li'l Cutie

" I'M saving "

Make your

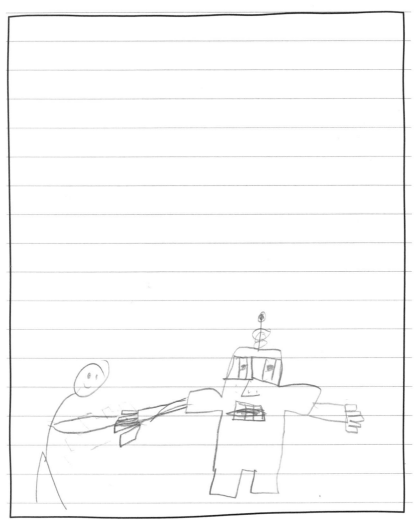

" My robot frend **"**

OWN comics

" NO Mine dork "

The FIRST FOUR LAWS you'll pass when you get elected president

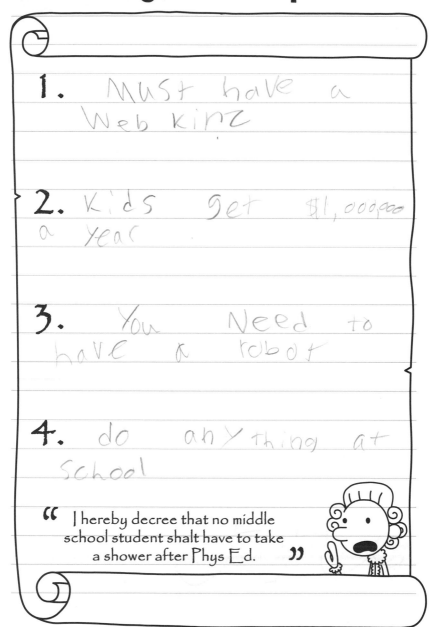

1. Must have a Web kinz

2. Kids get $1,000,000 a year

3. You Need to have a robot

4. do anything at School

" I hereby decree that no middle school student shalt have to take a shower after Phys Ed. "

The BADDEST THING
you ever did as a little kid

I talkled a
girl Because I
hated her guts

Practice your SIGNATURE

You'll be famous one day, so let's face it . . . that signature of yours is gonna need some work. Use this page to practice your fancy new autograph.

Tyler Ferry

Tyler Ferry

Tyler Ferry

Tyler

Ferry

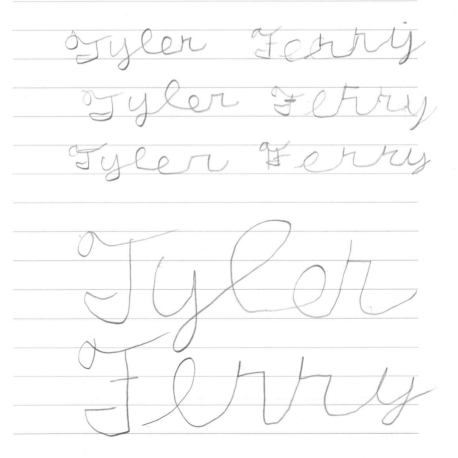

List your INJURIES

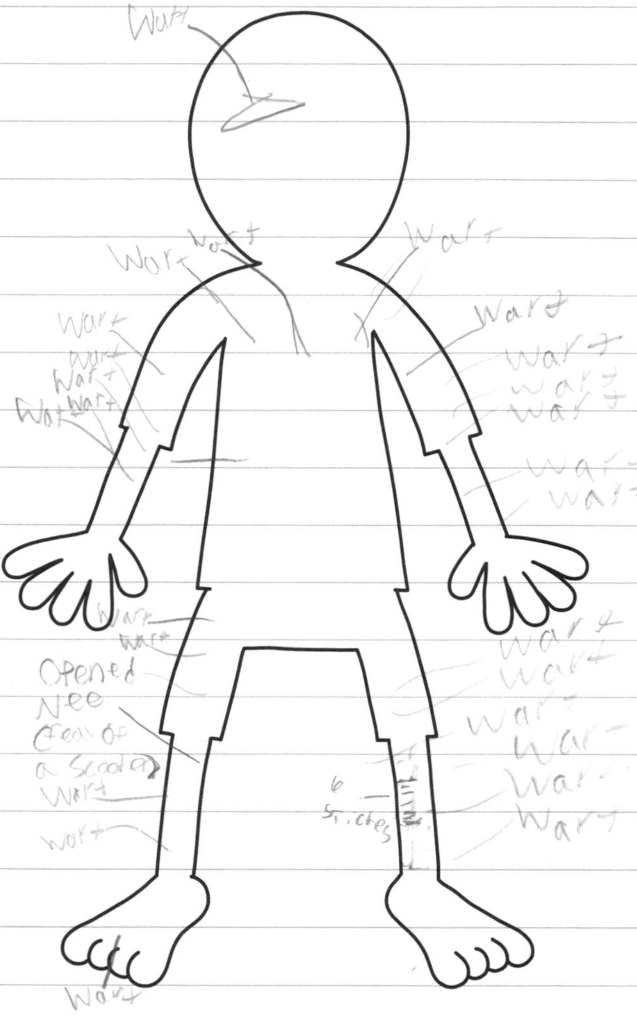
Wart
6 stitches

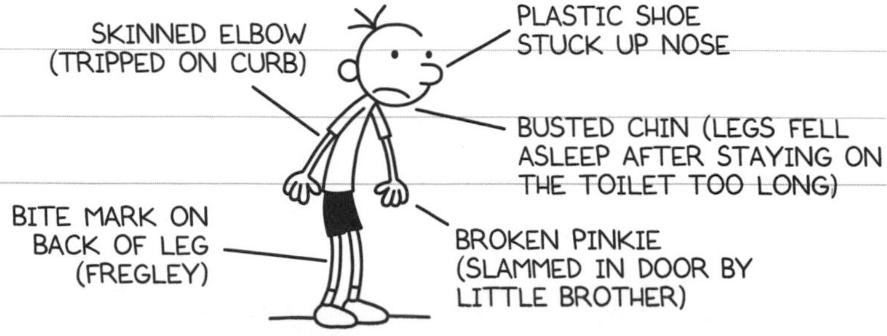
SKINNED ELBOW
(TRIPPED ON CURB)
PLASTIC SHOE
STUCK UP NOSE
BUSTED CHIN (LEGS FELL
ASLEEP AFTER STAYING ON
THE TOILET TOO LONG)
BITE MARK ON
BACK OF LEG
(FREGLEY)
BROKEN PINKIE
(SLAMMED IN DOOR BY
LITTLE BROTHER)

A few questions

Do you believe in unicorns?

NO

If you ever got to meet a unicorn, what would you ask it?

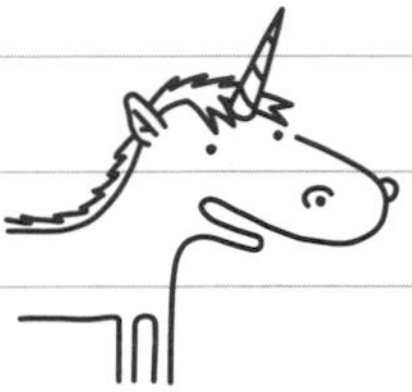

can I ride on you

Have you ever drawn a picture that was so scary that it gave you nightmares?

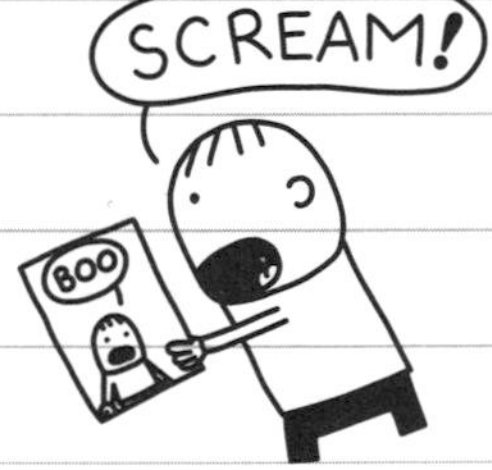
SCREAM!
BOO

yes

How many nights a week do you sleep in your parents' bed?

2 days

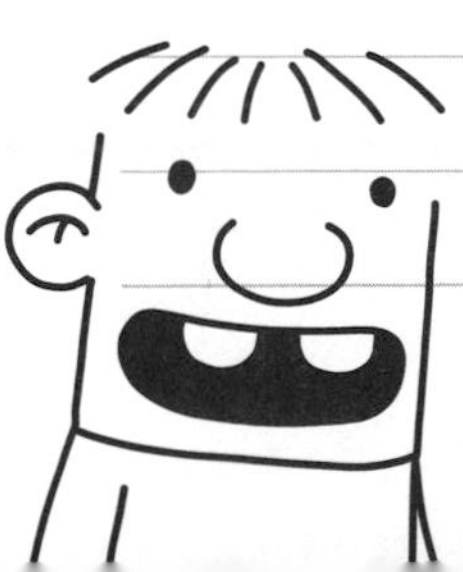

from ROWLEY 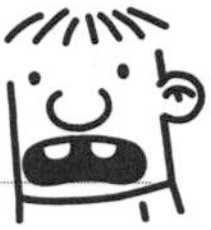

Have you ever tied your shoes without help from a grown-up?

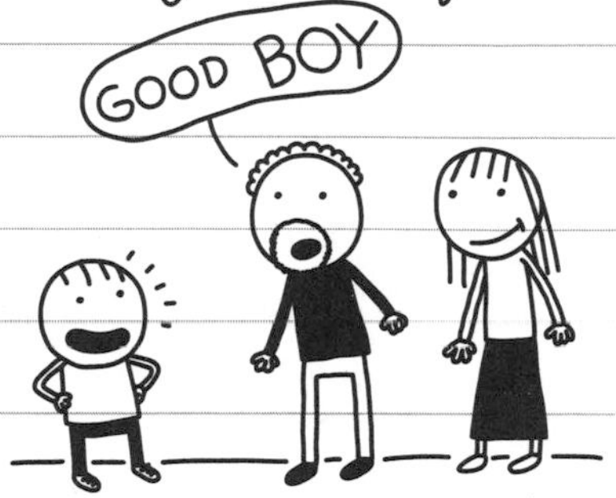
GOOD BOY

yes

Have you ever gotten sick from eating cherry lip gloss?

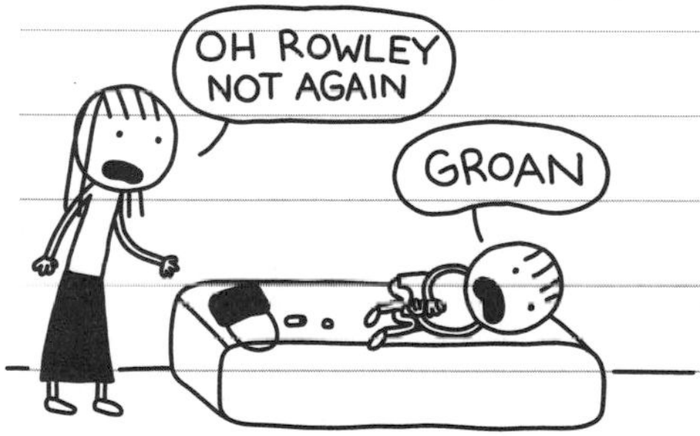
OH ROWLEY NOT AGAIN
GROAN

NO

Are your friends jealous that you're a really good skipper?

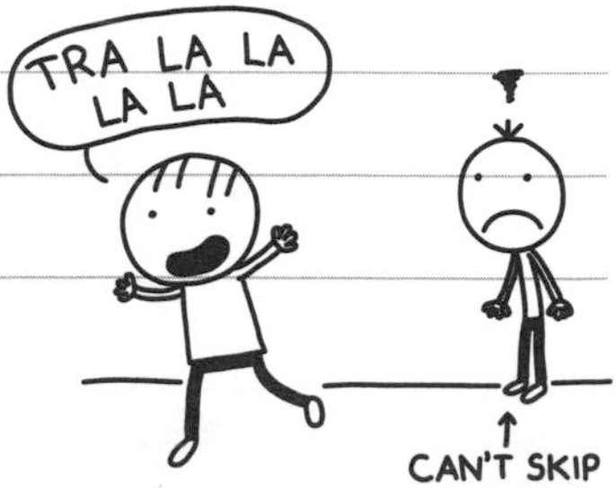
TRA LA LA LA LA
CAN'T SKIP

No

The BIGGEST MISTAKES

1. Believing my older brother when he said it was "Pajama Day" at my school.

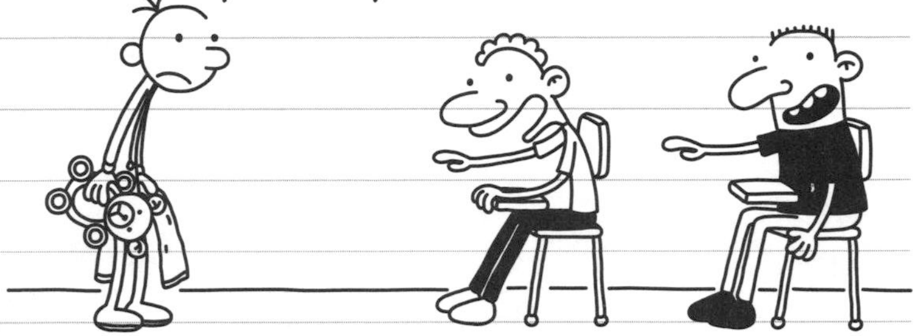

2. Taking a dare that probably wasn't worth it.

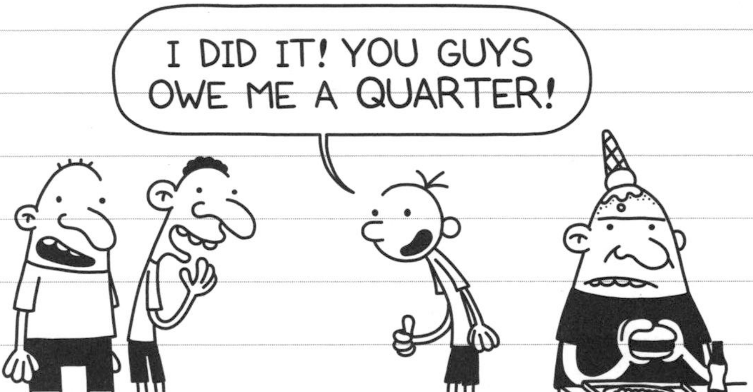
I DID IT! YOU GUYS OWE ME A QUARTER!

3. Giving Timmy Brewer my empty soda bottle.

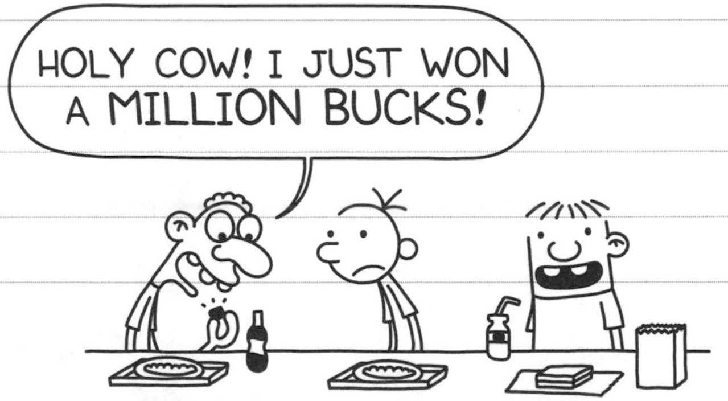
HOLY COW! I JUST WON A MILLION BUCKS!

you've made so far

1. I wore My Mom's glasses (with hearts) to School

2. I was butt Naked oN a trapaline at someones house

3. I was naked and home sick and My MoM opened the shades

Unfinished

Creighton the Cretin

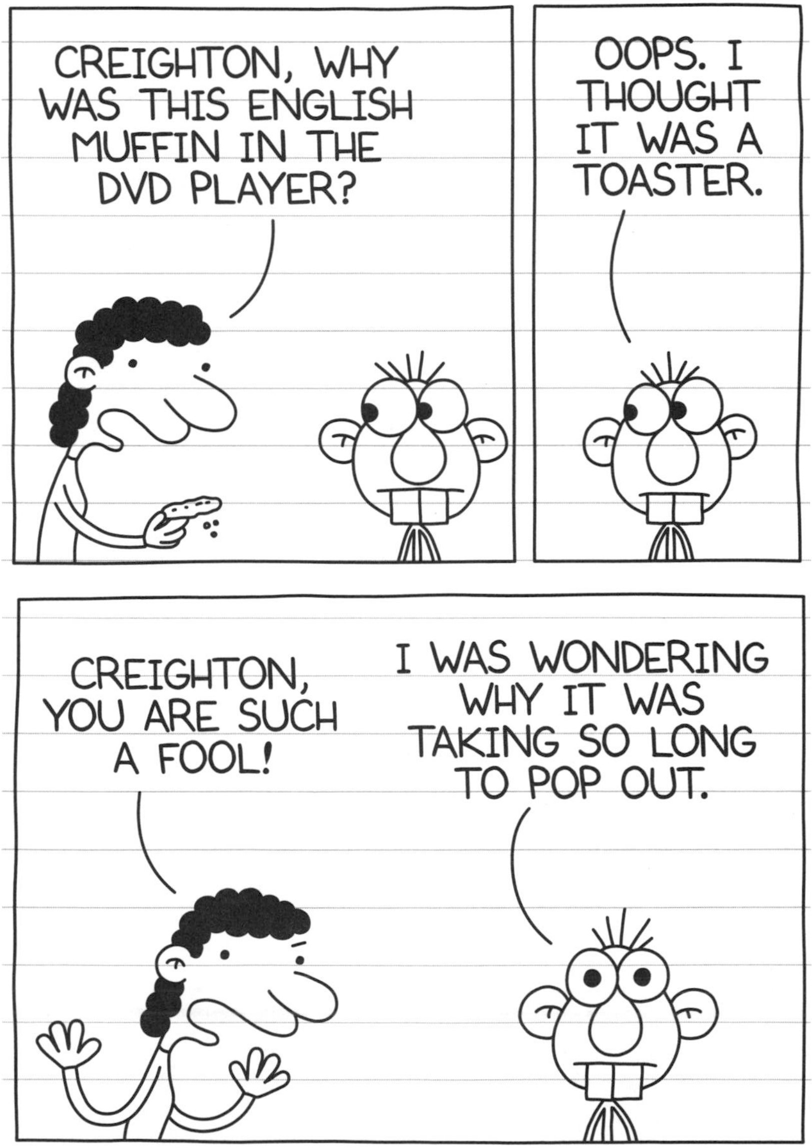

CREIGHTON, WHY WAS THIS ENGLISH MUFFIN IN THE DVD PLAYER?
OOPS. I THOUGHT IT WAS A TOASTER.
CREIGHTON, YOU ARE SUCH A FOOL!
I WAS WONDERING WHY IT WAS TAKING SO LONG TO POP OUT.

COMICS

Creighton the Cretin

I Put a english Maffin in the dvd Player
What
I Put a Maffin in the dvd Player
So What do You have to say
your are Very Stupid

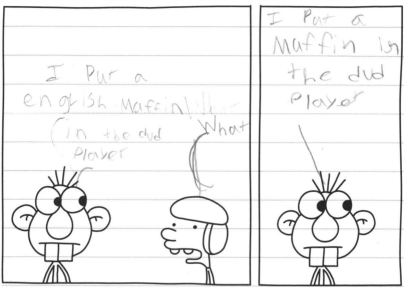

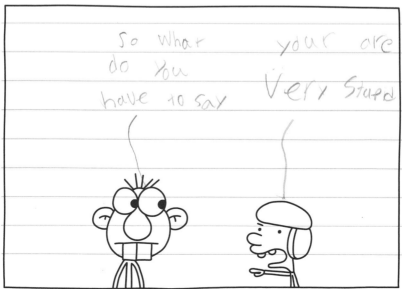

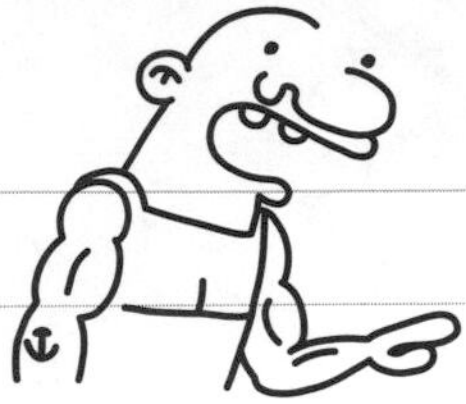

Make your

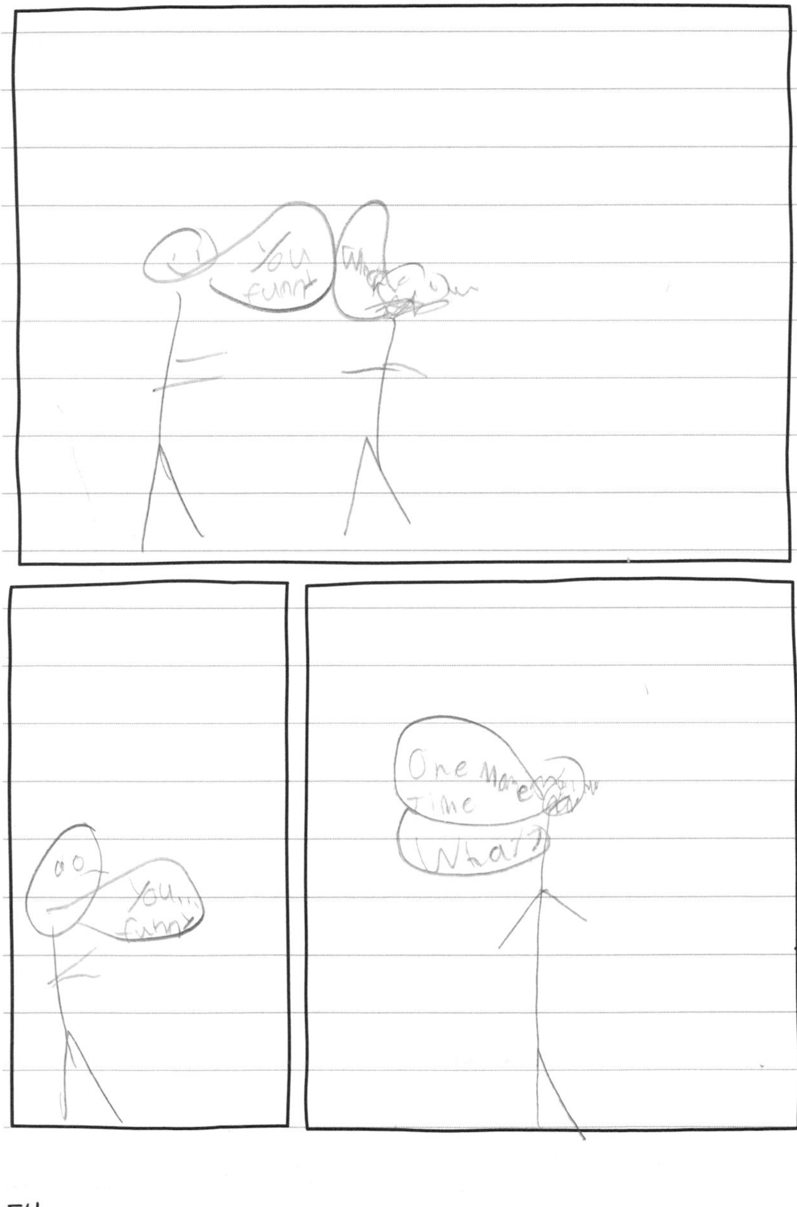

You funny
You... funny
One more time
What?

OWN comics

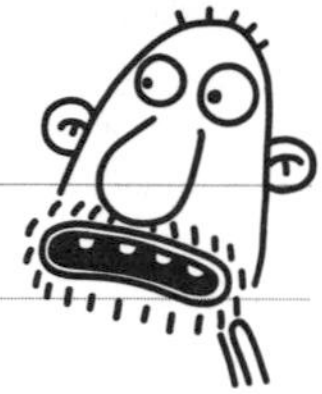

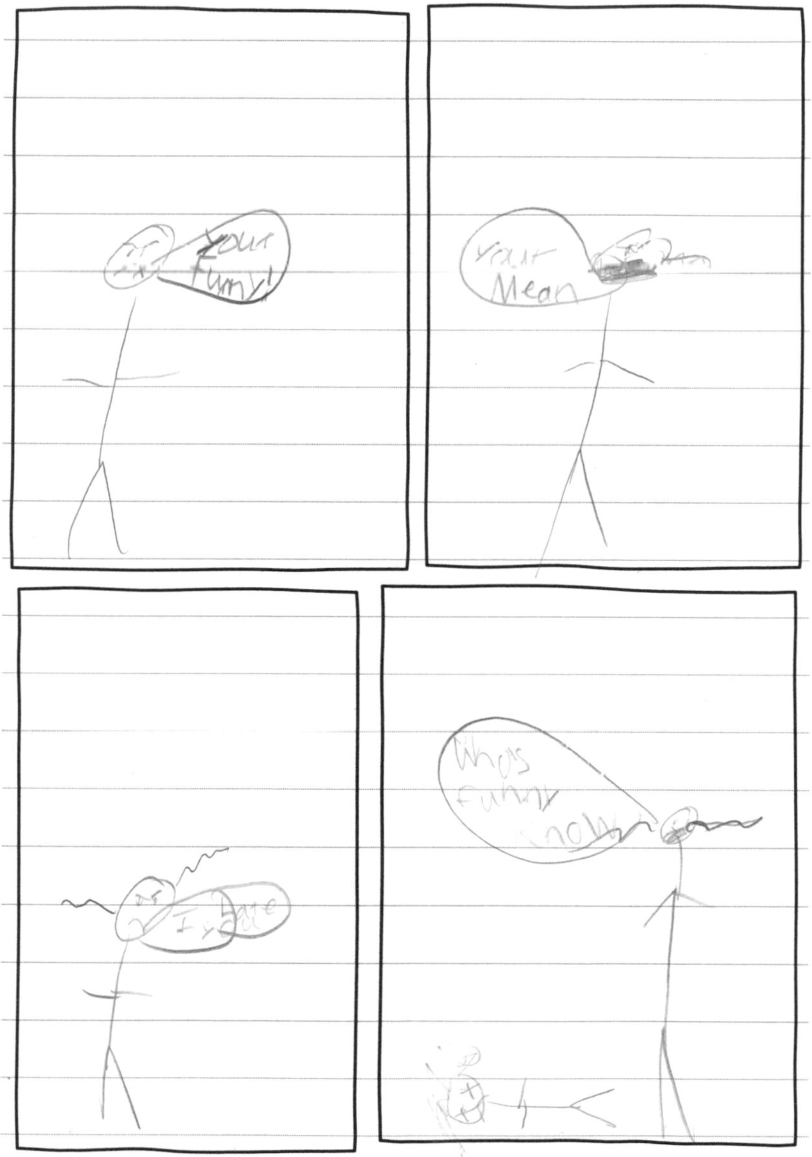
Your Funny!
Your Mean
I hate
Whos Funny Know

RODRICK'S

<u>INTELLIGENCE TESTER:</u>

Do this maze and then check to see if you're dumb or smart.

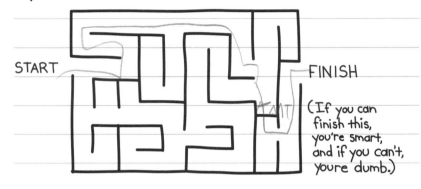

START

FINISH

(If you can finish this, you're smart, and if you can't, you're dumb.)

Put this sentence up to a mirror and then read it as loud as you can:

.ИОЯOM A MA I

Fill in the blank below:

Q: Who is awesome?

A: RODR_CK

(Hint: "I")

ACTIVITY PAGES

Answer this question yes or no <u>only</u>:

Q: Are you embarrassed that you pooped in your diaper today?

yes

Do you want to start a band? Well I guess you're out of luck because the best name is already taken and that's Löded Diper. But if you still want to start a band then you can use this mix-and-match thing: *

FIRST HALF
Wikkid
Nästy
Vilent
Rabbid
Killer
Ransid

SECOND HALF
Lizzerd
Pigz
Vömmit
Dagger
Syckle
Smellz

* P.S. If you use one of these names you owe me a hundred bucks.

How well do you

Answer these questions, and then ask your friend the same things. Keep track of how many answers you got right.

FRIEND'S NAME: _Austin_

Has your friend ever gotten carsick?   _yes_

If your friend could meet any celebrity, who would it be?   _Luccus (fred)_

Where was your friend born?   _texas_

Has your friend ever laughed so hard that milk came out of their nose?   _yes_

Has your friend ever been sent to the principal's office?   _Yes_

9–10: YOU KNOW YOUR FRIEND SO WELL IT'S SCARY
6–8: NOT BAD...YOU KNOW YOUR FRIEND PRETTY WELL!

know your FRIEND?

What's your friend's favorite
junk food?   choclate

Has your friend ever broken
a bone?   yes

When was the last time your
friend wet the bed?   a years

If your friend had to
permanently transform into
an animal, what animal would
it be?   deer

Is your friend secretly
afraid of clowns?   No

Now count up your correct answers and look at the
scale below to see how you did.

2–5: DID YOU GUYS JUST MEET OR SOMETHING?
0–1: TIME TO GET A NEW FRIEND

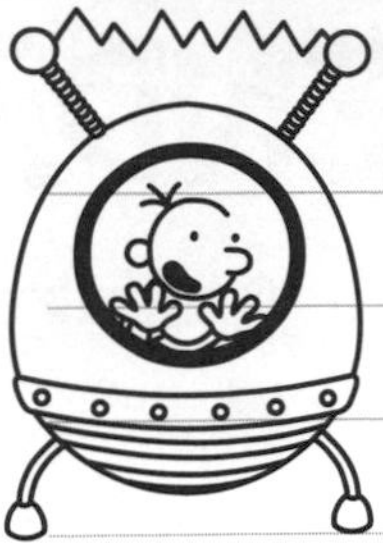

If you had a

If you could go back in time and change the future, but you only had five minutes, where would you go?

Save Myself
FrOM getting a CuBcusoin

If you could go back in time and witness any event in history, what would it be?

She how King
tut died

If you had to be stuck living in some time period in the past, what time period would you pick?

Yesterday

TIME MACHINE...

If you could go back and videotape one event from your own life, what would it be?

When my cosin wished for something and it came true

If you could go back and tell your past self one thing, what would it be?

don't dig a hole, you know the one by the oak tree so you don't get a concusin

If you could go forward in time and tell your future self something, what would it be?

Your so cool because your from the futre

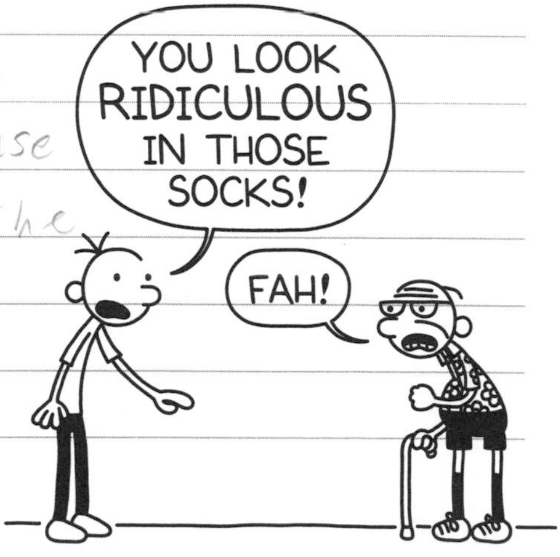

YOU LOOK RIDICULOUS IN THOSE SOCKS!
FAH!

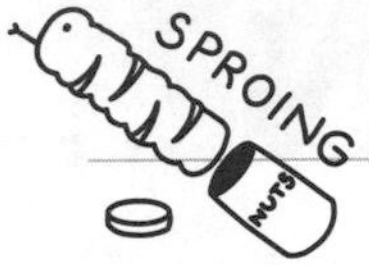
SPROING
NUTS

Totally awesome

The "Stand on One Foot" trick

STEP ONE: On your way home from school, bet your friend they can't stand on one foot for three minutes without talking.

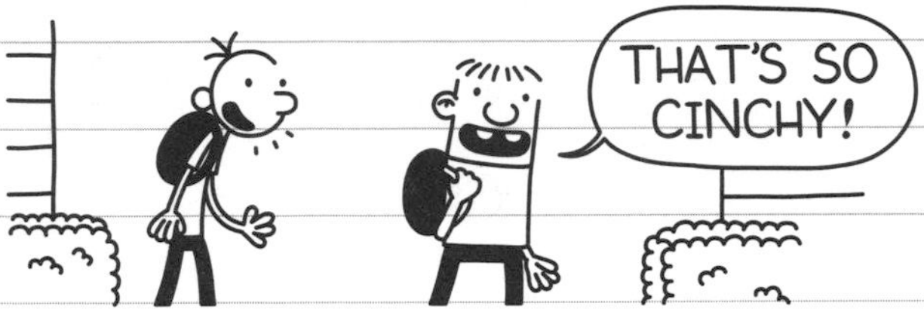
THAT'S SO CINCHY!

STEP TWO: While your friend stands on one foot, knock real hard on some crabby neighbor's front door.

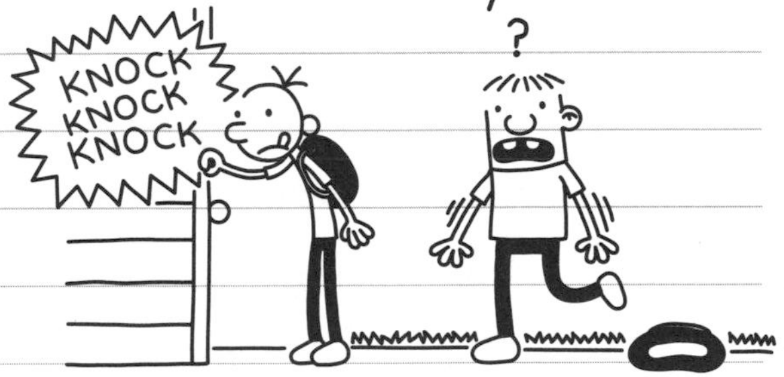
KNOCK KNOCK KNOCK
?

STEP THREE: Run.

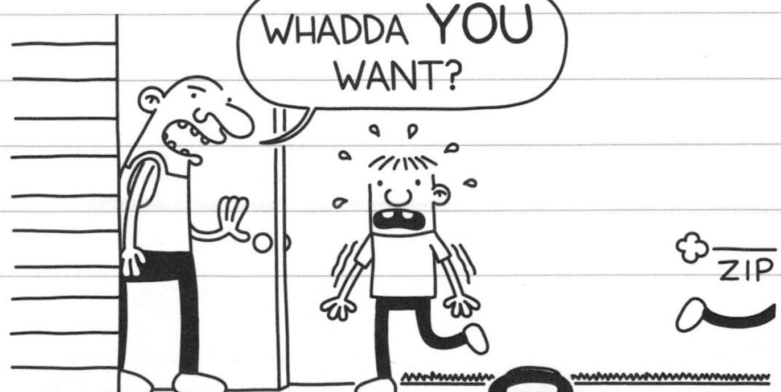
WHADDA YOU WANT?
ZIP

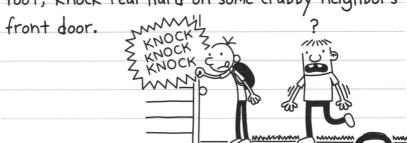

PRACTICAL JOKES

A JOKE YOU'VE PLAYED ON A FRIEND:

I shuk up on
them and tackled
them

A JOKE YOU'VE PLAYED ON A FAMILY MEMBER:

I snuk up on them
and scared them.

A JOKE YOU'VE PLAYED ON A TEACHER:

I Put a Whopee
cushon on ter her
chair

Your DRESSING

If you end up being a famous musician or a movie star, you're gonna need to put together a list of things you'll need in your dressing room.

Requirements for Greg Heffley - page 1 of 9

3 liters of grape soda

2 extra-large pepperoni pizzas

2 dozen freshly baked chocolate chip cookies

1 bowl of jelly beans (no pink or white ones)

1 popcorn machine

1 52-inch plasma TV

3 video game consoles with 10 games apiece

1 soft-serve ice cream machine

10 waffle cones

1 terry-cloth robe

1 pair of slippers

*** bathroom must have heated toilet seat

*** toilet paper must be name brand

ROOM requirements

You might as well get your list together now so that you're ready when you hit the big time.

1 Mansion
2 Pets

3 Liters of soda

4 77-inch plasma tv
78 arcade games

79 room

407,978,492 - square inches

Unfinished

The Amazing Fart Police

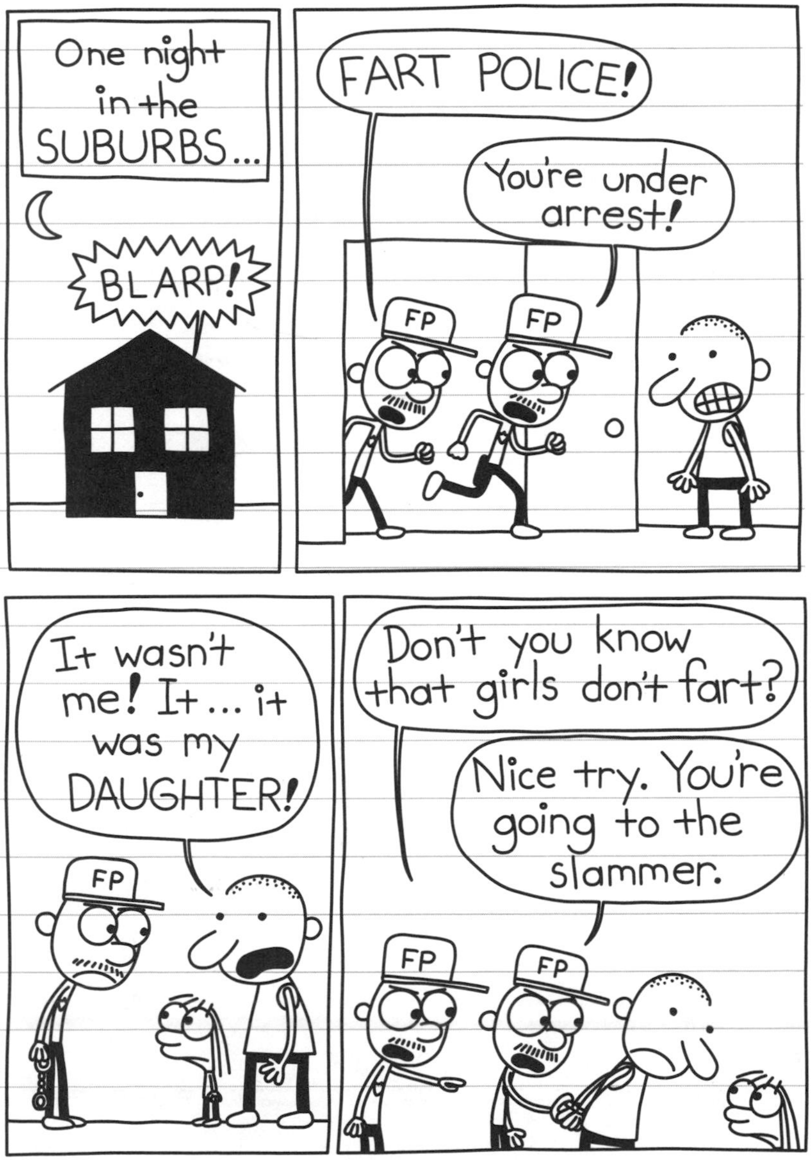

One night in the SUBURBS...
BLARP!
FART POLICE!
You're under arrest!
It wasn't me! It... it was my DAUGHTER!
Don't you know that girls don't fart?
FP
Nice try. You're going to the slammer.

COMICS

The Amazing Fart Police

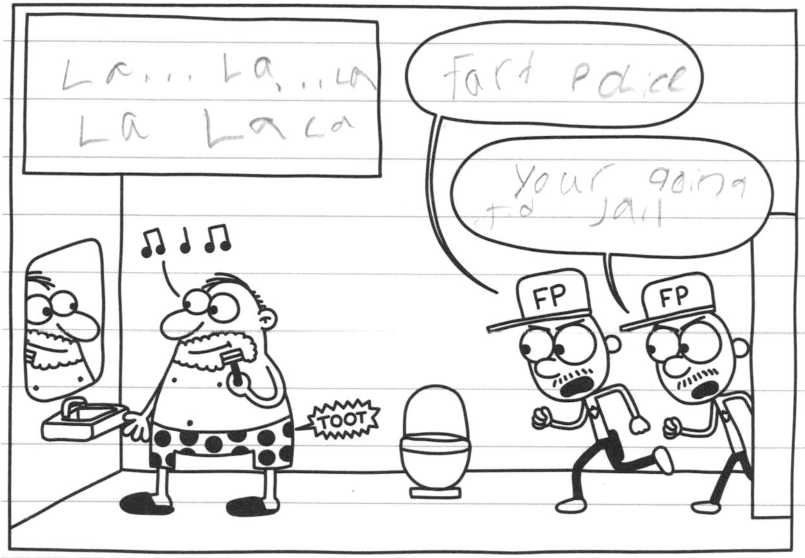
La... La... La
La Laca
Fart police
your going to jail
TOOT

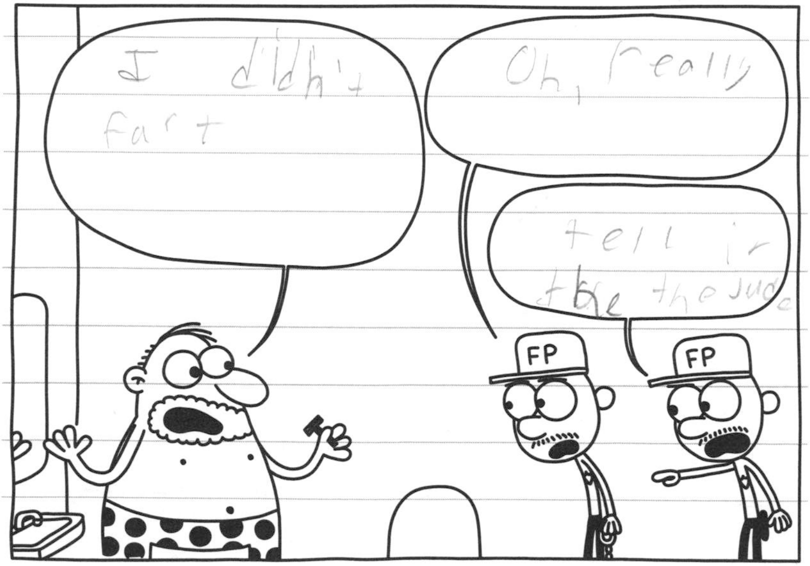
I didn't fart
Oh, really
tell it

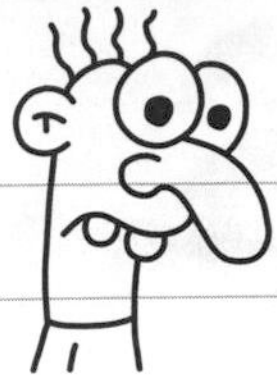

Make your

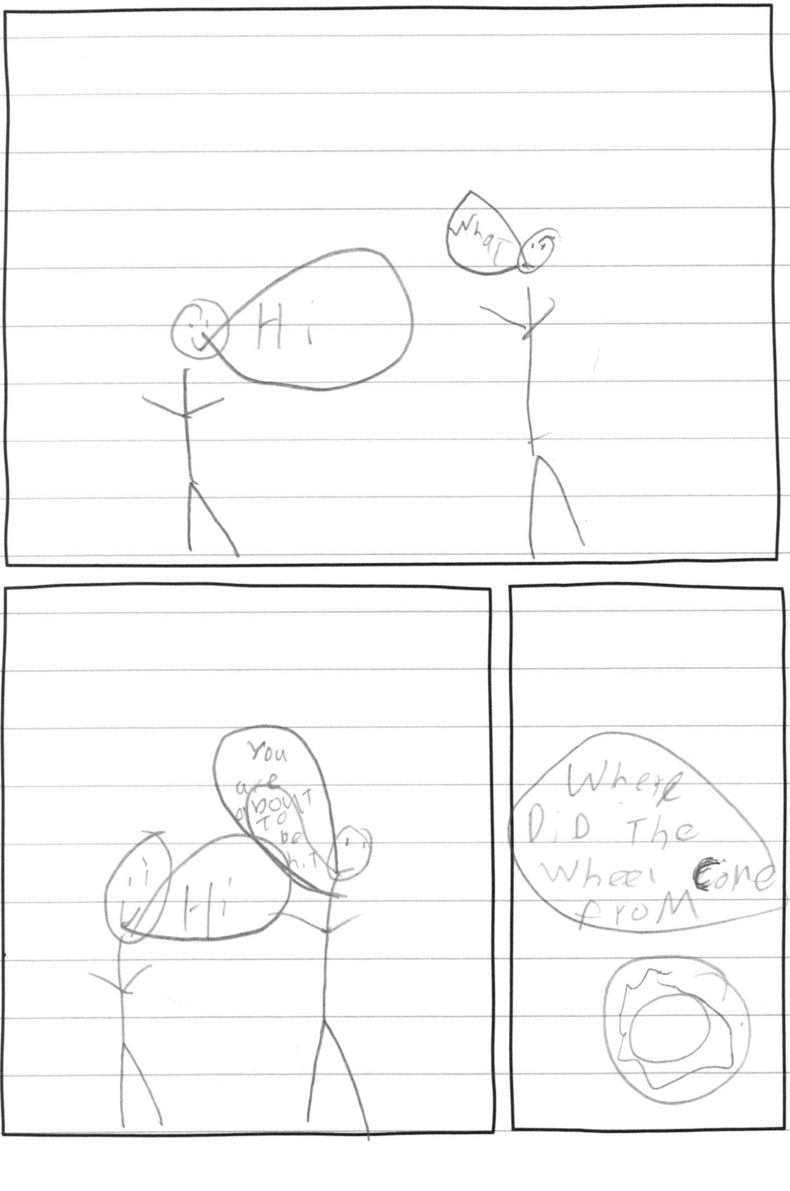
Hi
What
Hi
You are about To be hiT
Where Did The Wheel Come from

OWN comics

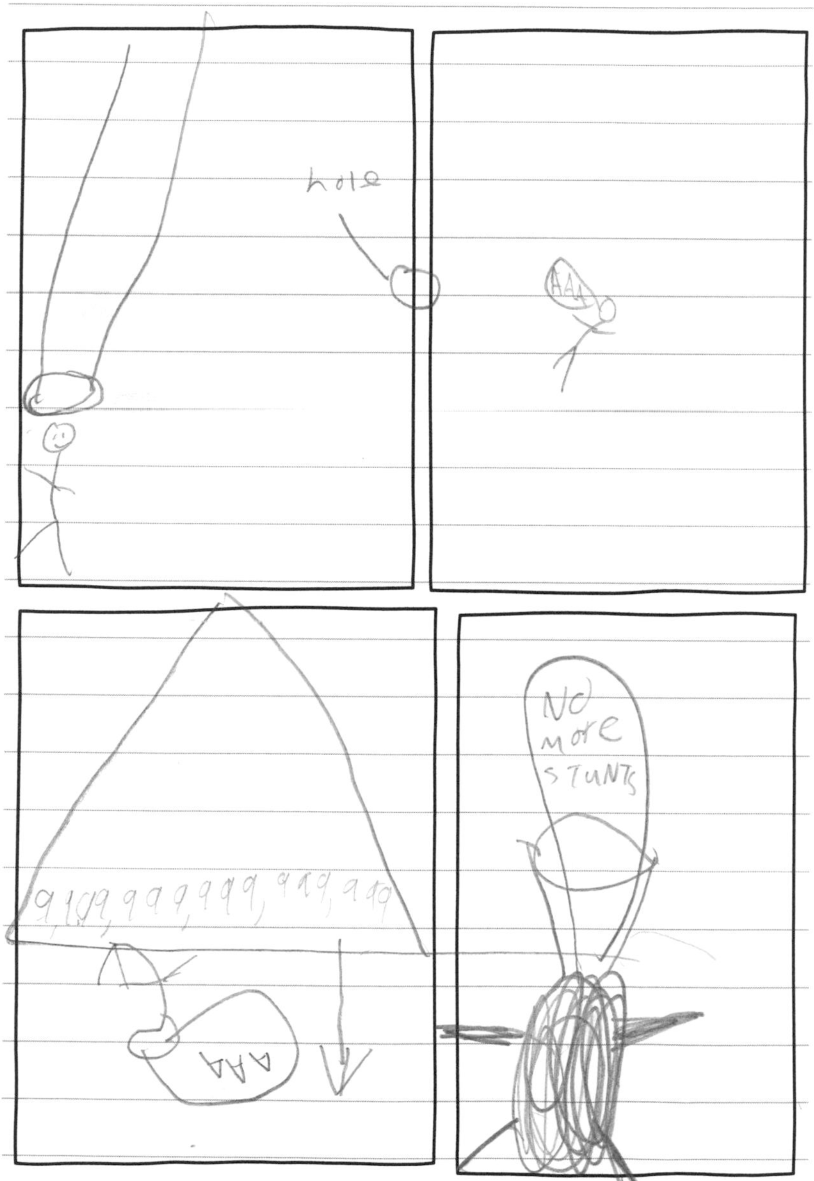
hole
NO more STUNTS

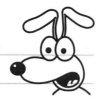

Your best ideas for

BAD-BREATH DEFLECTOR

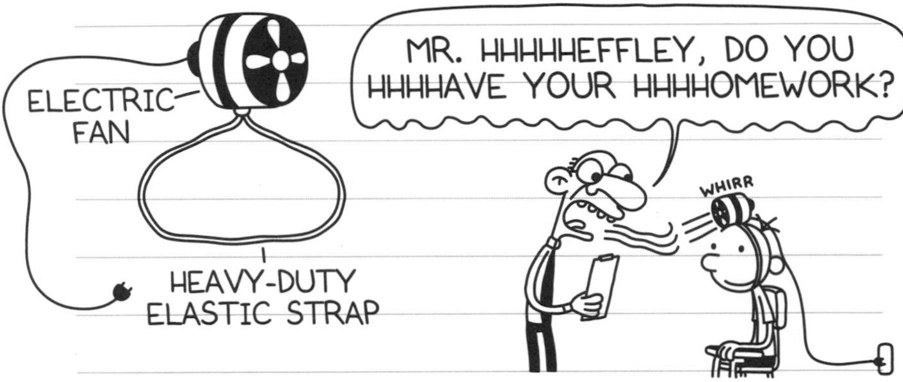
ELECTRIC FAN
HEAVY-DUTY ELASTIC STRAP
MR. HHHHHEFFLEY, DO YOU HHHHAVE YOUR HHHHOMEWORK?
WHIRR

ANIMAL TRANSLATOR

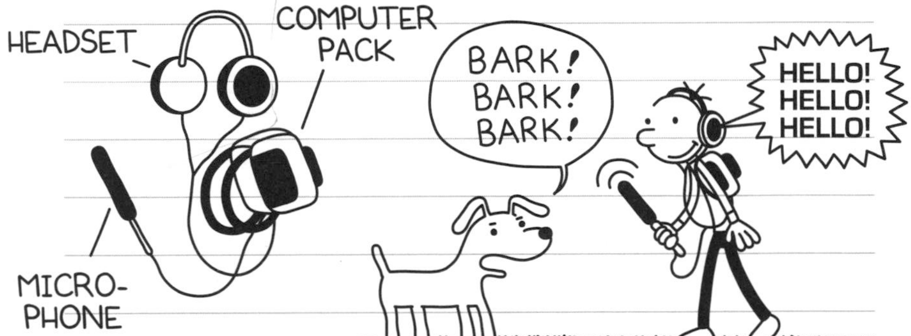
HEADSET
COMPUTER PACK
MICRO-PHONE
BARK! BARK! BARK!
HELLO! HELLO! HELLO!

FLAVOR STICK

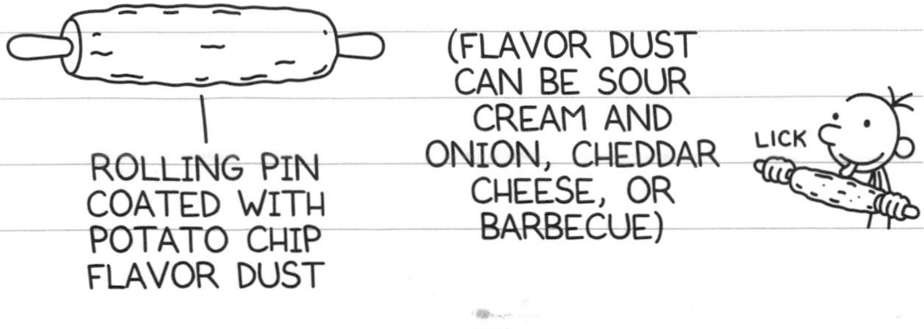
ROLLING PIN COATED WITH POTATO CHIP FLAVOR DUST
(FLAVOR DUST CAN BE SOUR CREAM AND ONION, CHEDDAR CHEESE, OR BARBECUE)
LICK

INVENTIONS

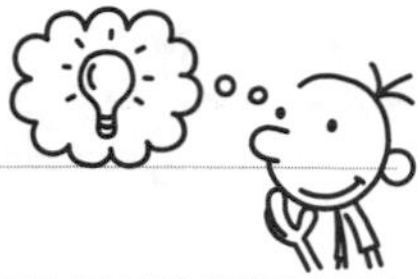

WRITE DOWN YOUR OWN AWESOME IDEAS SO YOU CAN PROVE YOU CAME UP WITH THEM BEFORE ANYONE ELSE.

MiND reader

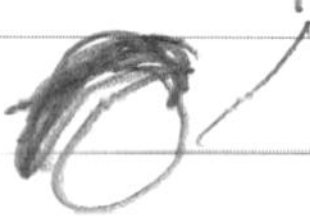

The flYer

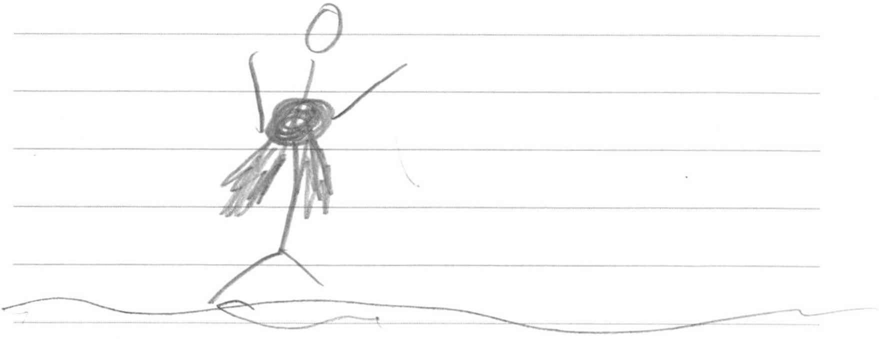

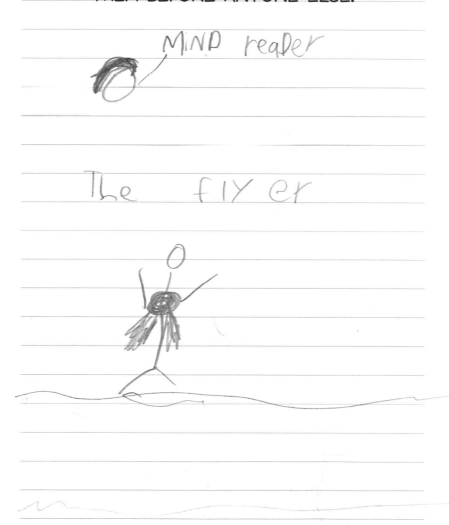

Make a map of your

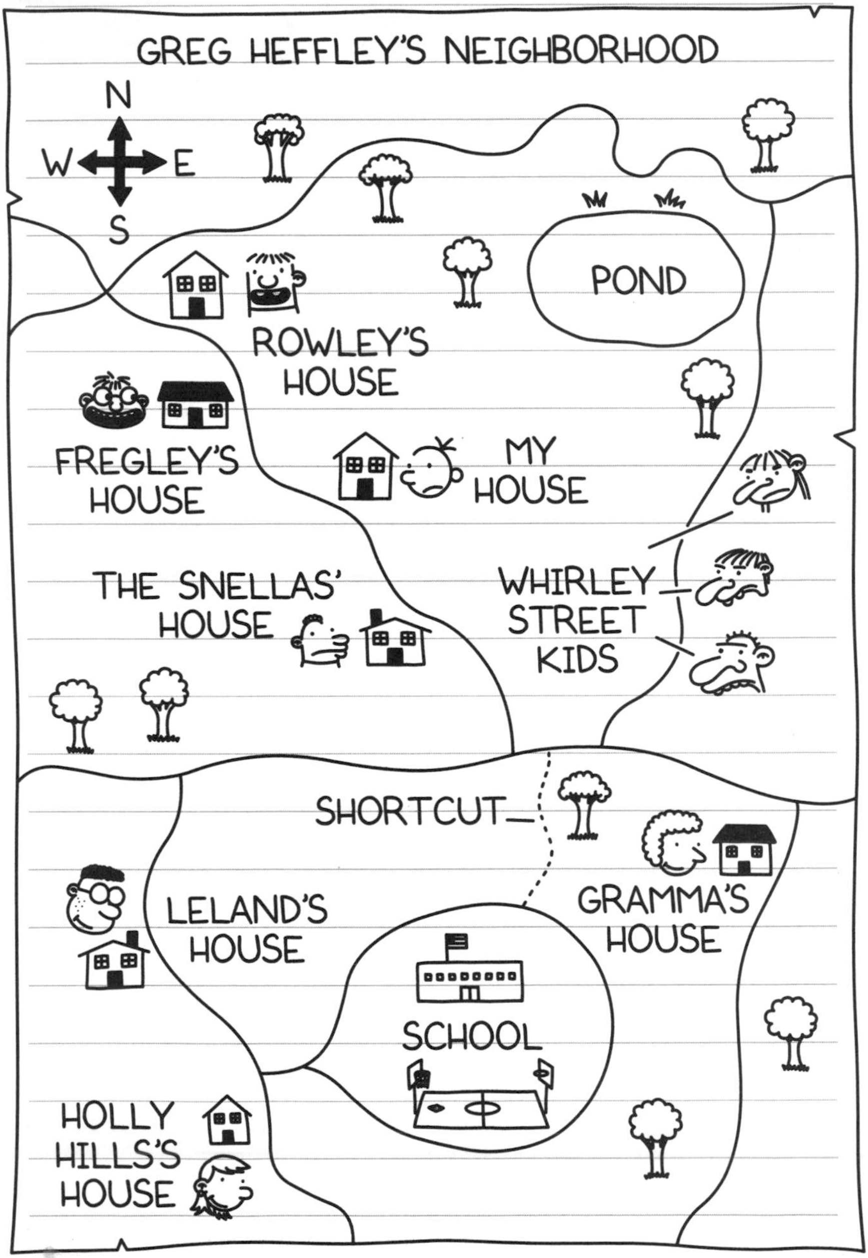
GREG HEFFLEY'S NEIGHBORHOOD
N
W
E
S
POND
ROWLEY'S HOUSE
FREGLEY'S HOUSE
MY HOUSE
THE SNELLAS' HOUSE
WHIRLEY STREET KIDS
SHORTCUT
GRAMMA'S HOUSE
LELAND'S HOUSE
SCHOOL
HOLLY HILLS'S HOUSE

NEIGHBORHOOD

YOUR NEIGHBORHOOD

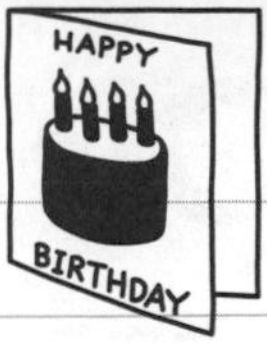
HAPPY
BIRTHDAY

Make your own

FRONT

Dear Aunt Jean,

THANK YOU

for the wonderful socks you knitted for me.

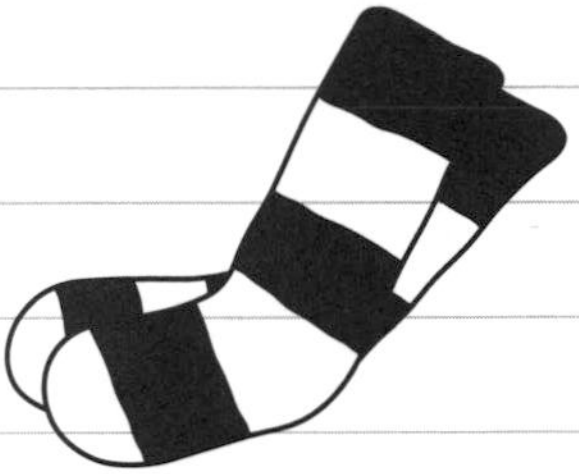

INSIDE

But next time, could we just stick with cash?

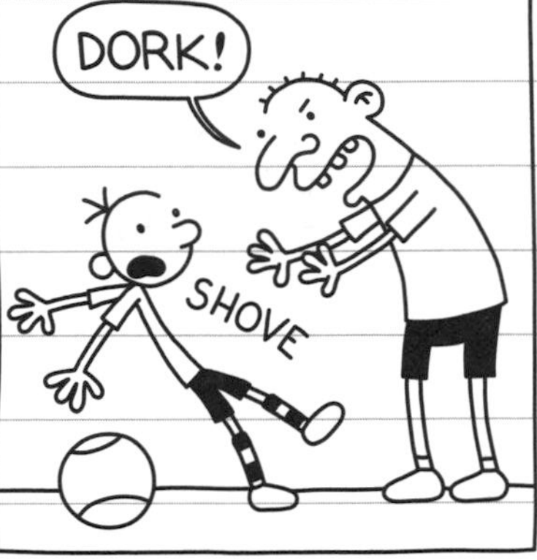
DORK!
SHOVE

FRONT

I'm sorry

that it didn't work out with you and Lyndsey.

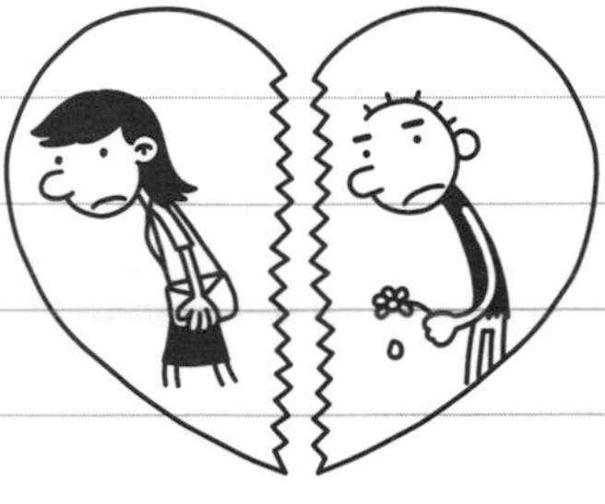

INSIDE

P.S. Could you find out if she thinks I'm "cute"?

GREETING CARDS

FRONT

I am

am selling
cool items

INSIDE

You
have To
Pay
MoNey

$ Chuching $

FRONT

I Rock

INSIDE

ouT
Loud

The BEST VACATION
you ever went on

I loved when
I went to the
great wolf
Lodge. I want to
save up to bye
a wand and book

That's it.
STOP MOKING ME

by,
Tyler

Make a LÖDED DIPER CONCERT POSTER

LODED DIPER

We ROCK
So MUCH

you CAN Thorw
STuff at US

ON OCTober
31st 2010

Unfinished

Xtreme Sk8ers

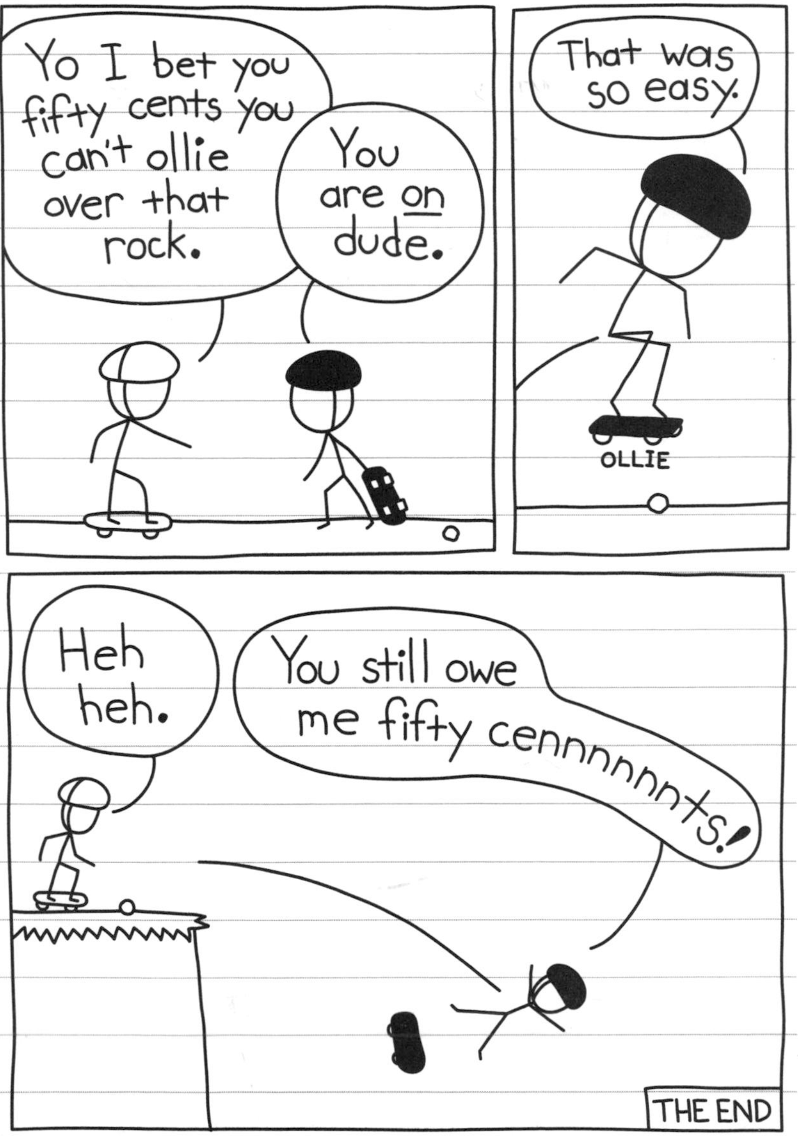
Yo I bet you fifty cents you can't ollie over that rock.
You are on dude.
That was so easy.
OLLIE
Heh heh.
You still owe me fifty cennnnnnnts!
THE END

COMICS

Xtreme Sk8ers

I bet you twenty five cents to ride down the ramp
Here we go.
NOT MY board
ahhh MONSTERS
THE END

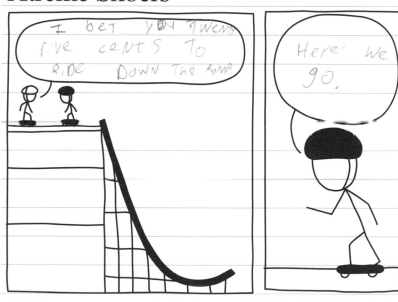

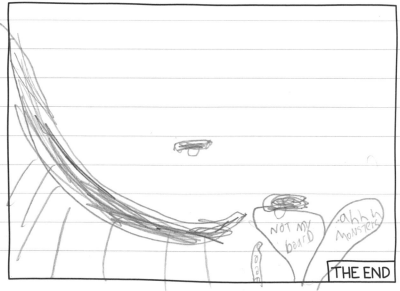

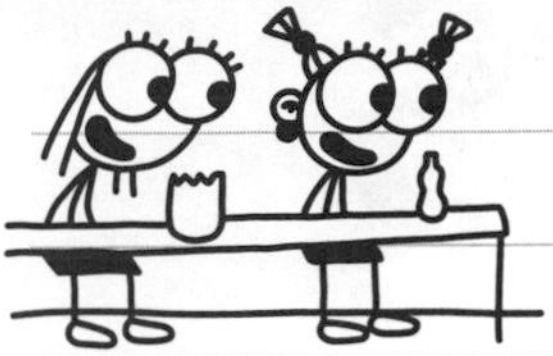

Make your

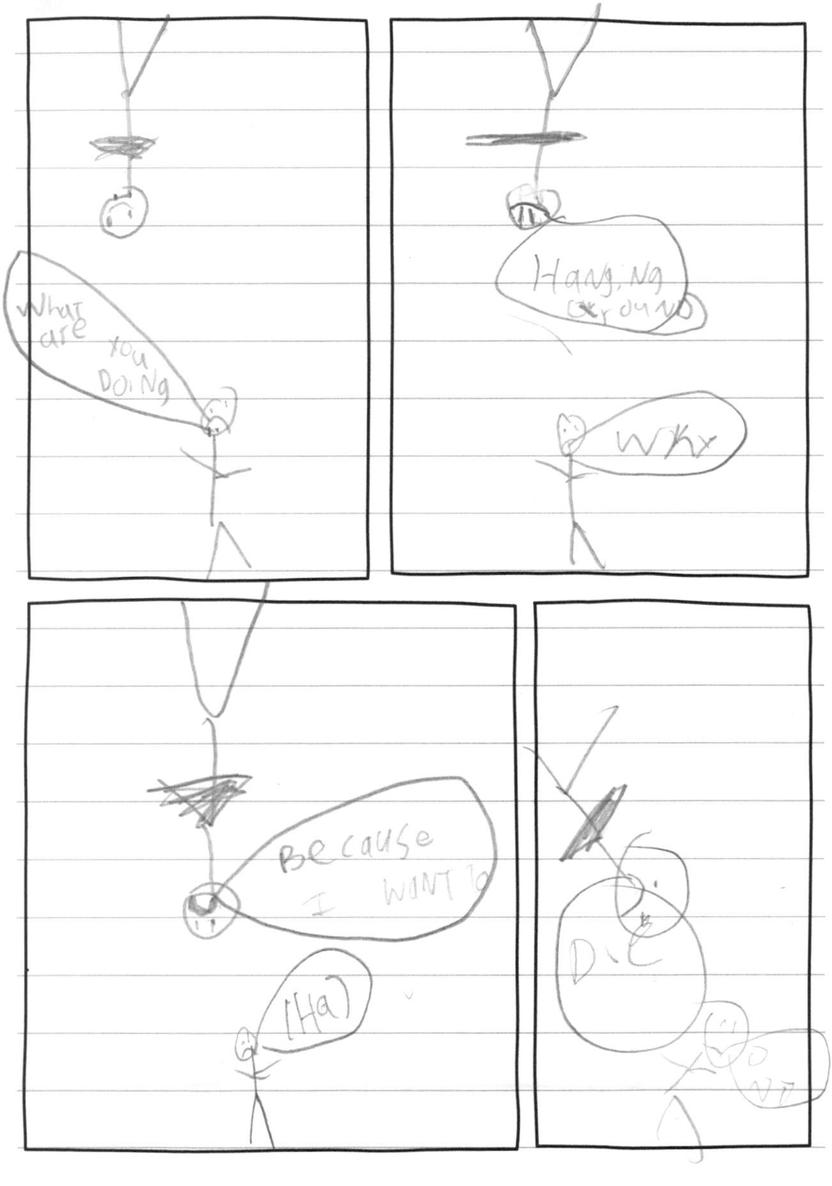
What are you Doing
Hanging
Why
Because I WANT to
Ha

OWN comics

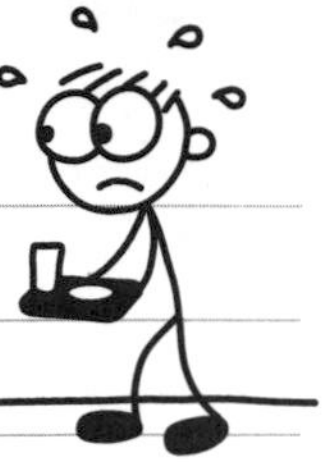

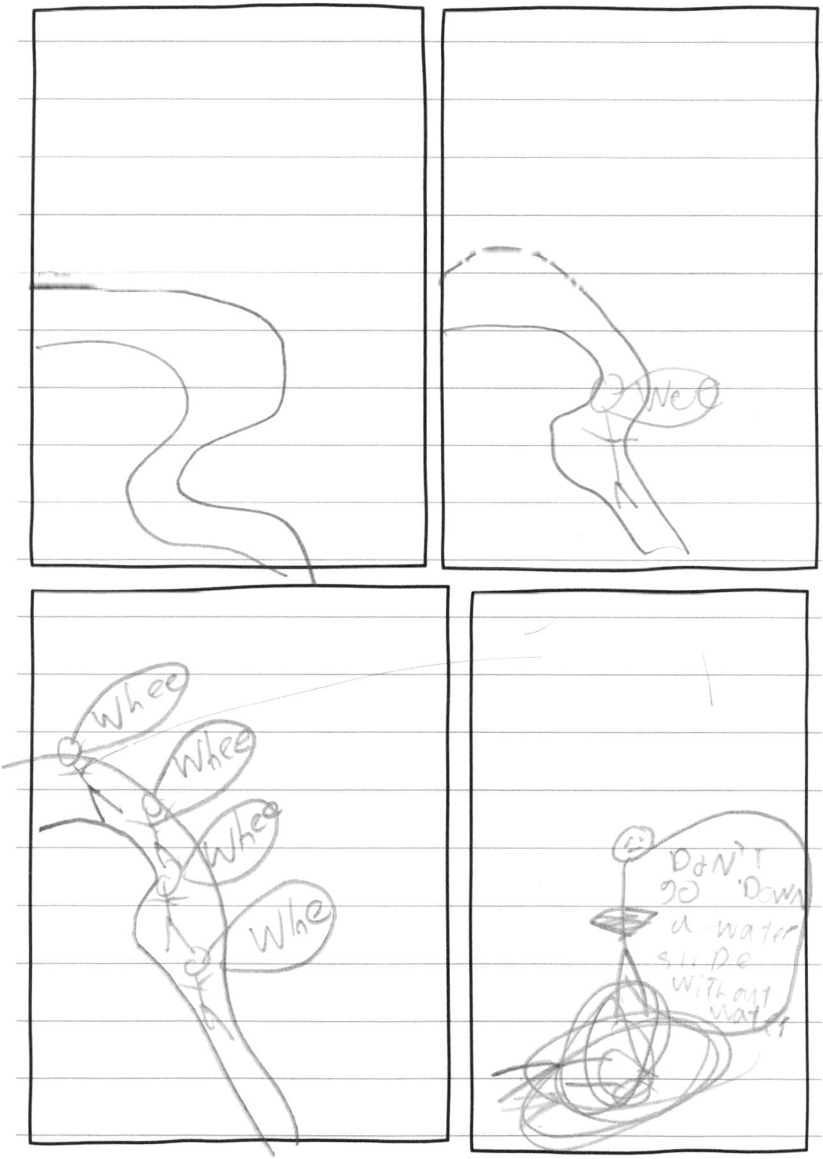
Whee
Whee
Whee
DON'T GO DOWN a water slide without water

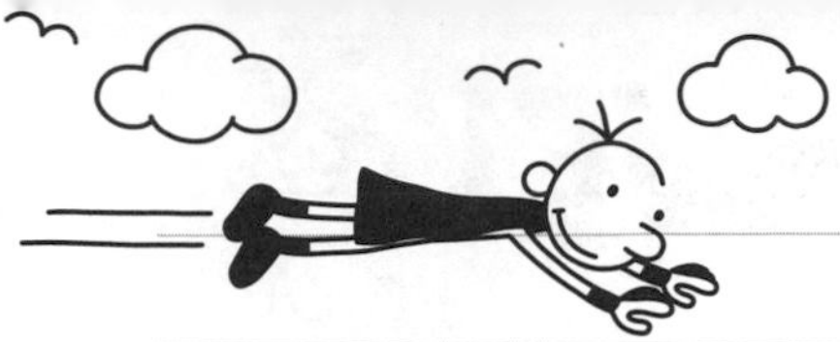

If you had

If you had the power to read other people's thoughts, would you really want to use it?

YES ☑ NO ☐

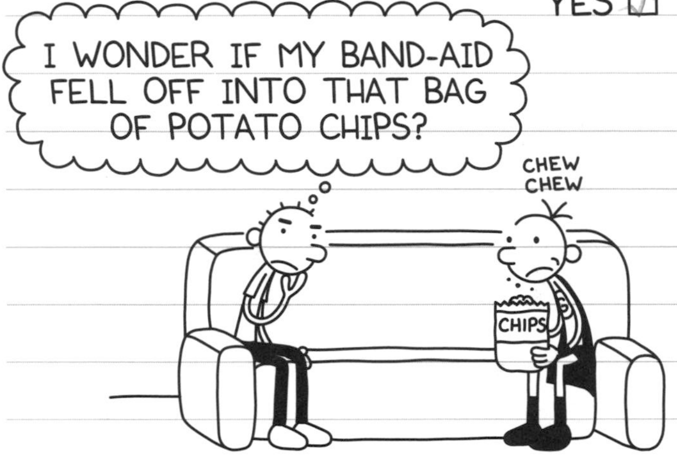

I WONDER IF MY BAND-AID FELL OFF INTO THAT BAG OF POTATO CHIPS?
CHEW CHEW
CHIPS

If you were a super hero, would you want to have a sidekick? YES ☑ NO ☐

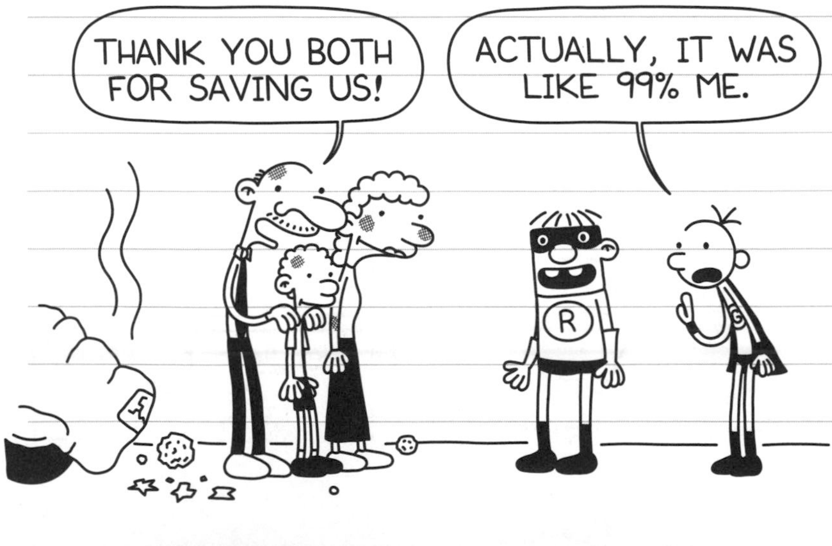

THANK YOU BOTH FOR SAVING US!
ACTUALLY, IT WAS LIKE 99% ME.
R

SUPERPOWERS...

If you were a super hero, would you keep your identity secret? YES ☑ NO ☐

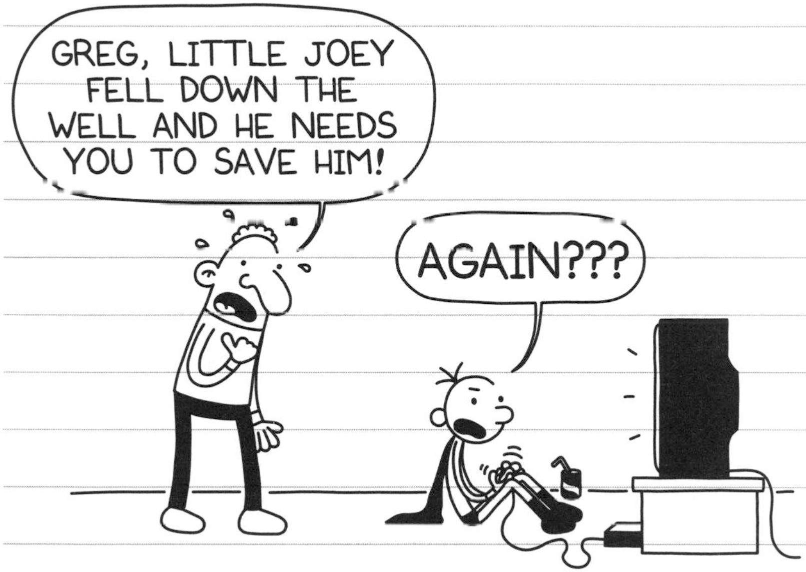
GREG, LITTLE JOEY FELL DOWN THE WELL AND HE NEEDS YOU TO SAVE HIM!
AGAIN???

Would you want to have X-ray vision if you couldn't turn it off? YES ☐ NO ☑

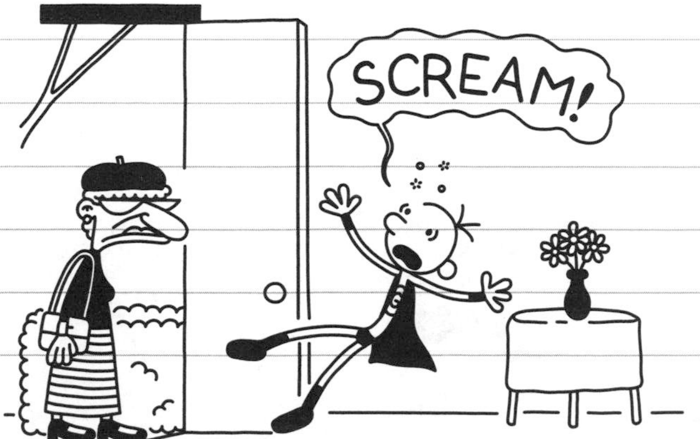
SCREAM!

Draw your FRIENDS

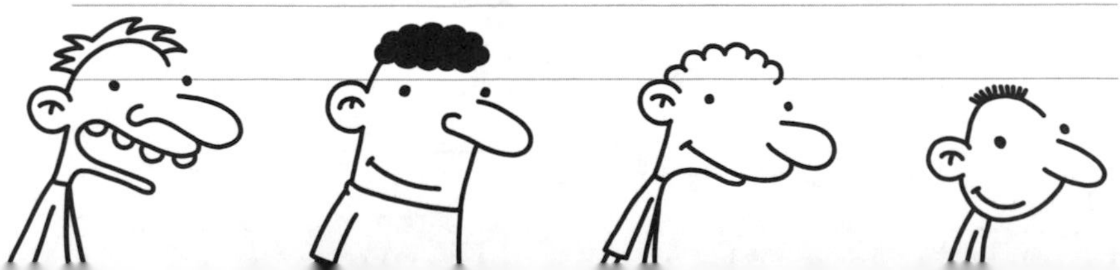

the way Greg Heffley would

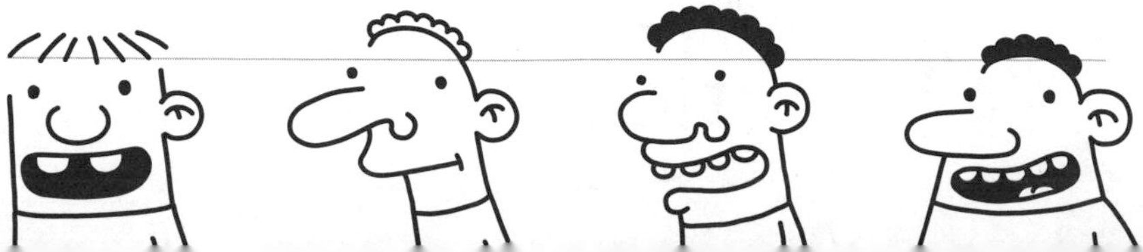

A few questions

Do you ever put food in your belly button so you can have a snack later on?

NO

Do animals ever use their thoughts to talk to you?

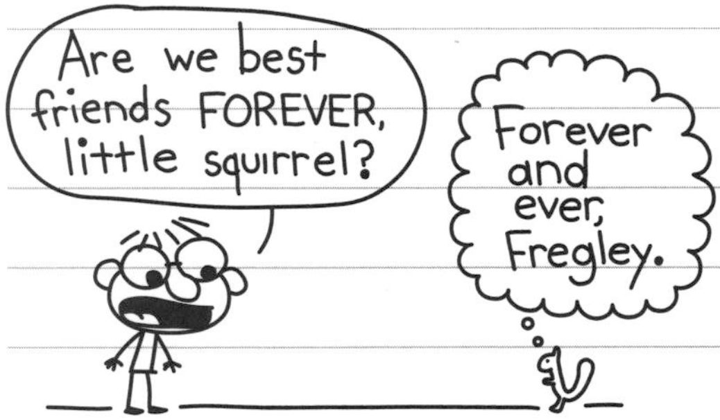
Are we best friends FOREVER, little squirrel?
Forever and ever, Fregley.

NO

Has your guidance counselor ever called you "unpredictable and dangerous"?

Yes

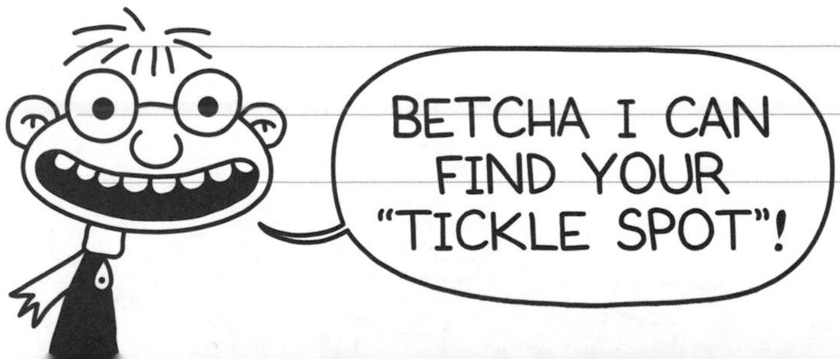
BETCHA I CAN FIND YOUR "TICKLE SPOT"!

from FREGLEY

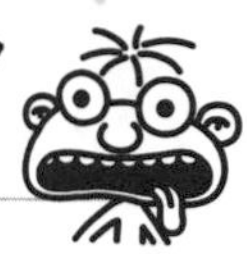

If you had a tail, what would you do with it?

wag iT.

Have you ever eaten a scab?

No

Do you wanna play "Diaper Whip"?

No

Have you ever been sent home from school early for "hygiene issues"?

No

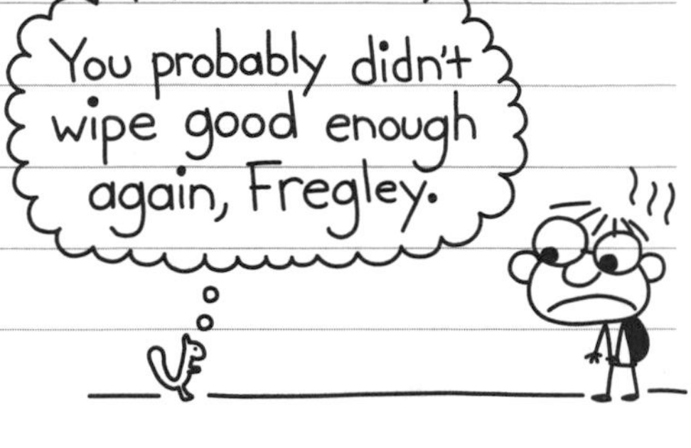
You probably didn't wipe good enough again, Fregley.

Autographs

GET YOUR FRIENDS TO WRITE STUFF IN THIS BOOK.

Lawson
Best bud forever

Michael
Best
friend
forever
you rock!

Autographs

ZOO-WEE MAMA by Rowley

Excuse me sir can I see your neck for a second?
Sure but how come?
Because I am a vampire!
CHOMP
ZOO-WEE MAMA!
Whew! I just had a bad dream that I was buried alive!
Aieee! I am buried alive!
R.I.P.
ZOO-WEE MAMA!
My new cloning gun can make copies of anything.
Aw...you're full of baloney.
ZAP
ZOO-WEE MAMA!

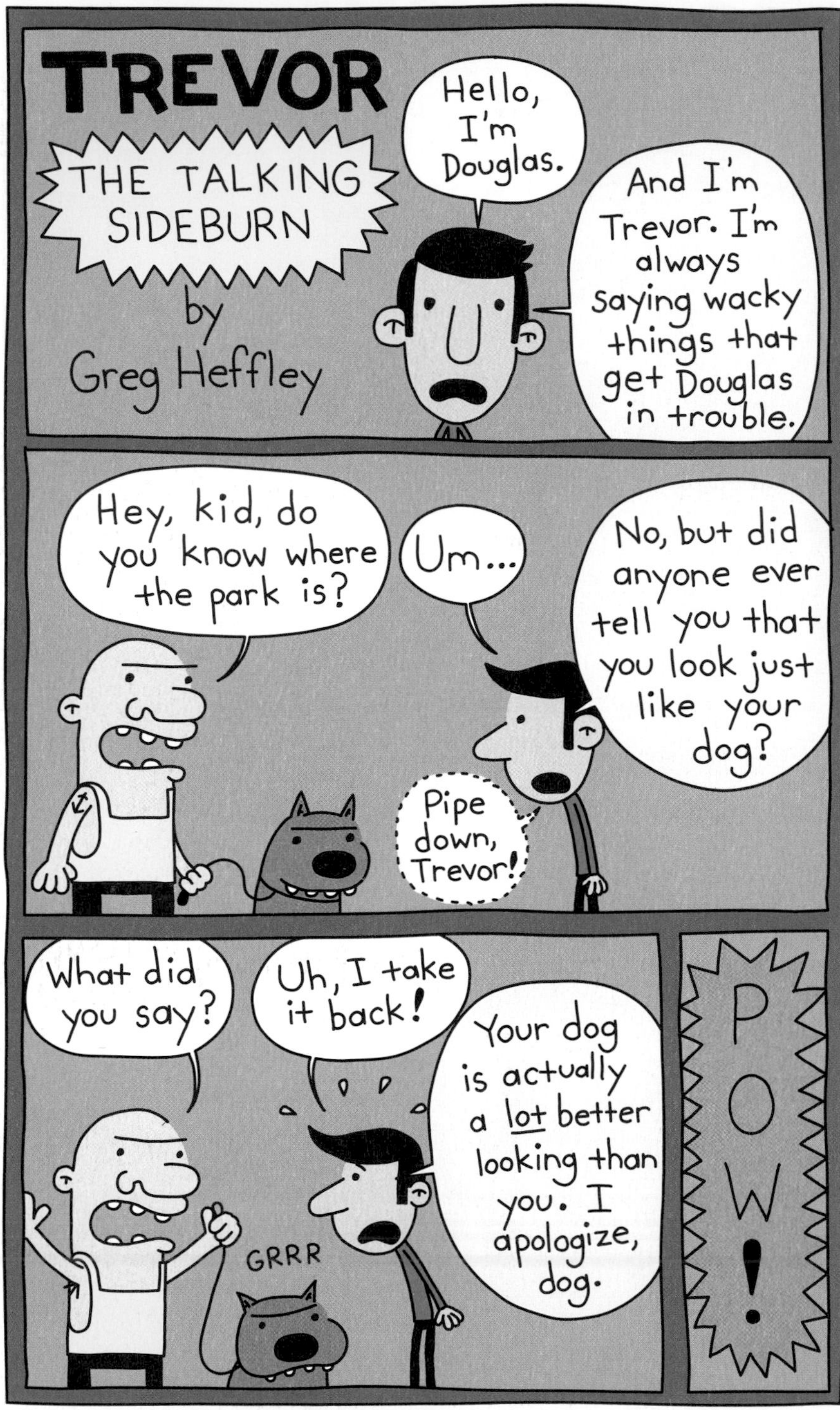
TREVOR
THE TALKING SIDEBURN
by Greg Heffley
Hello, I'm Douglas.
And I'm Trevor. I'm always saying wacky things that get Douglas in trouble.
Hey, kid, do you know where the park is?
Um...
No, but did anyone ever tell you that you look just like your dog?
Pipe down, Trevor!
What did you say?
Uh, I take it back!
Your dog is actually a lot better looking than you. I apologize, dog.
GRRR
POW!

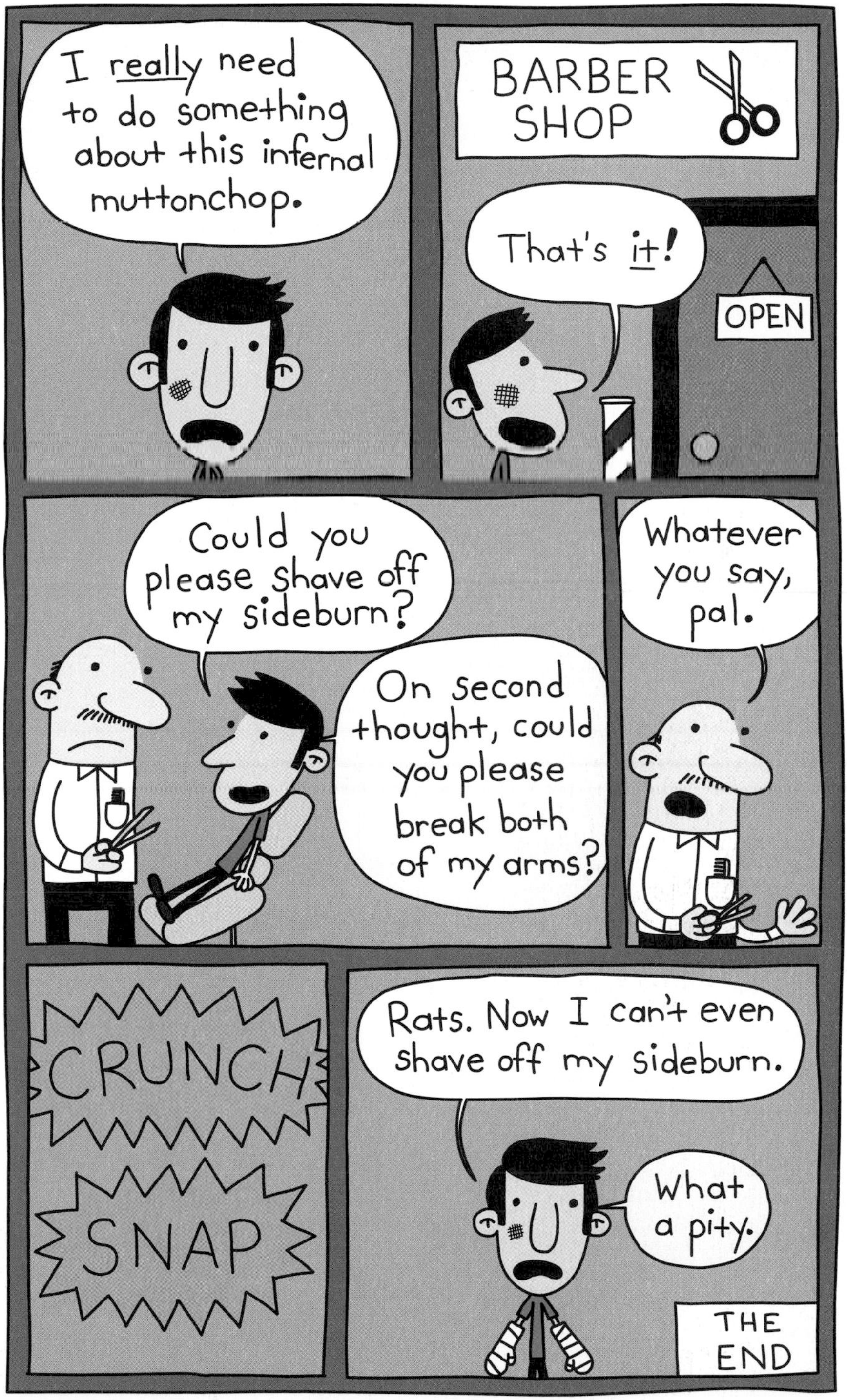

I really need to do something about this infernal muttonchop.
BARBER SHOP
That's it!
OPEN
Could you please shave off my sideburn?
On second thought, could you please break both of my arms?
Whatever you say, pal.
CRUNCH
SNAP
Rats. Now I can't even shave off my sideburn.
What a pity.
THE END

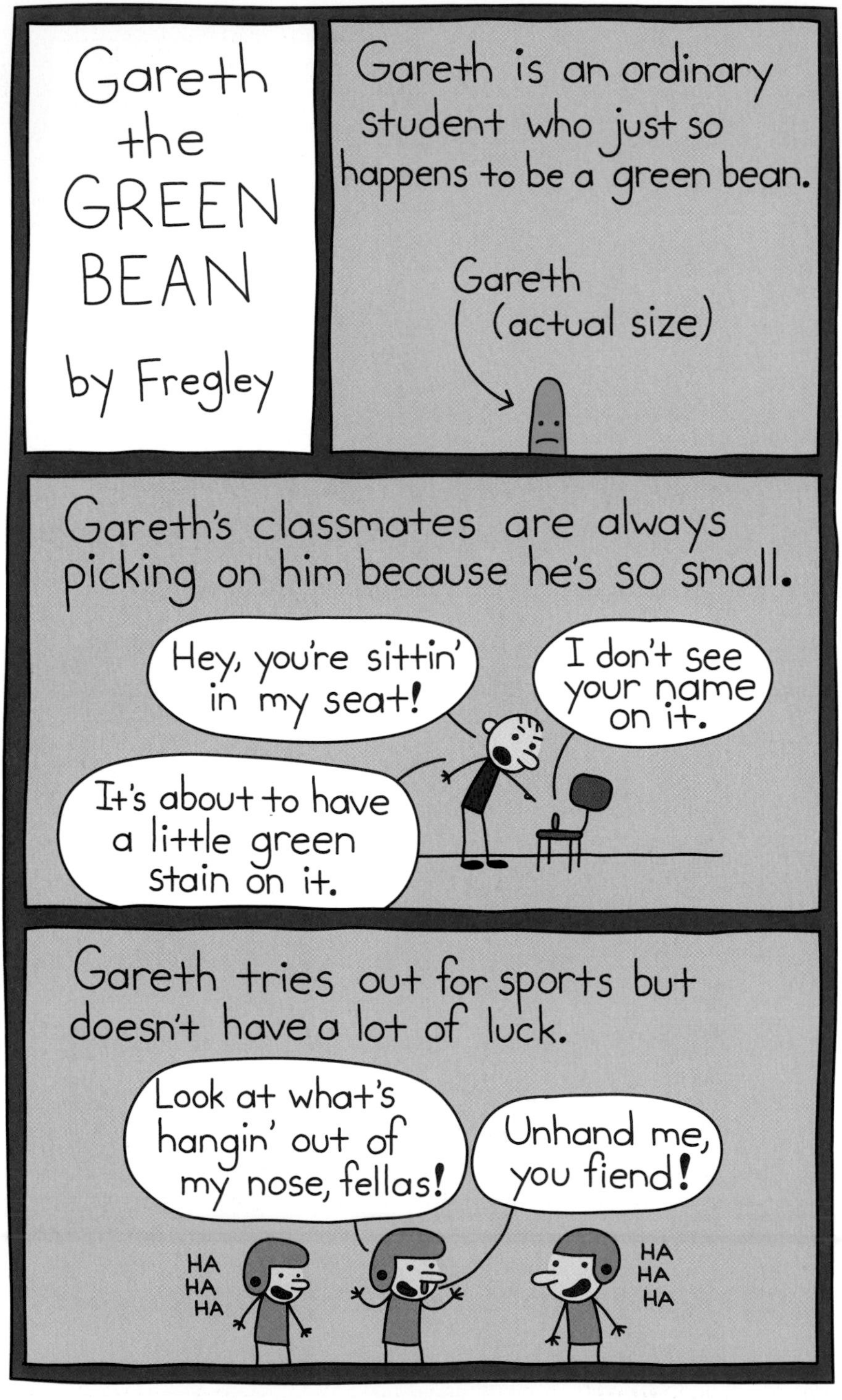
Gareth the GREEN BEAN
by Fregley
Gareth is an ordinary student who just so happens to be a green bean.
Gareth (actual size)
Gareth's classmates are always picking on him because he's so small.
Hey, you're sittin' in my seat!
I don't see your name on it.
It's about to have a little green stain on it.
Gareth tries out for sports but doesn't have a lot of luck.
Look at what's hangin' out of my nose, fellas!
Unhand me, you fiend!
HA HA HA
HA HA HA

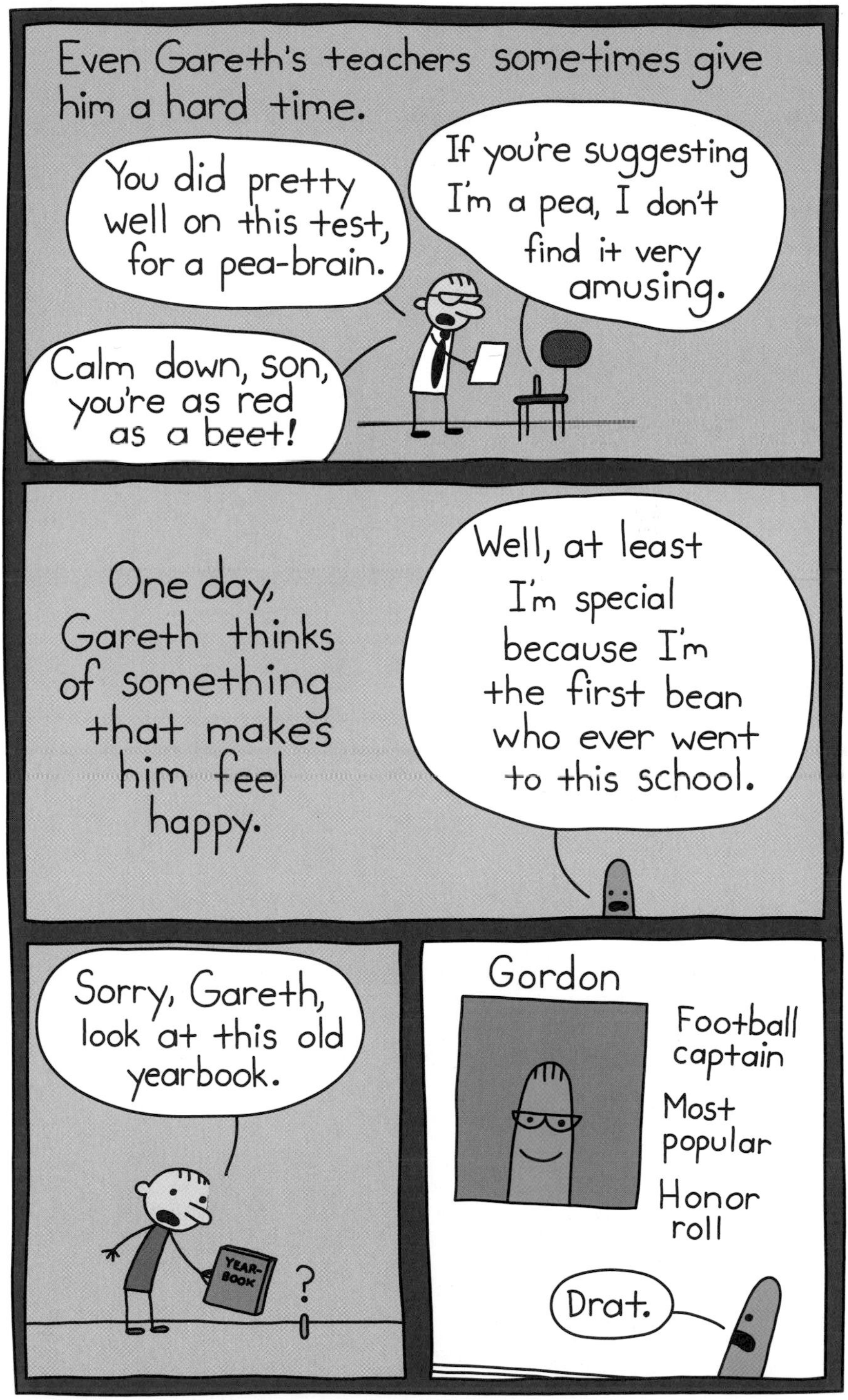

Even Gareth's teachers sometimes give him a hard time.
You did pretty well on this test, for a pea-brain.
If you're suggesting I'm a pea, I don't find it very amusing.
Calm down, son, you're as red as a beet!
One day, Gareth thinks of something that makes him feel happy.
Well, at least I'm special because I'm the first bean who ever went to this school.
Sorry, Gareth, look at this old yearbook.
YEAR-BOOK
?
Gordon
Football captain
Most popular
Honor roll
Drat.

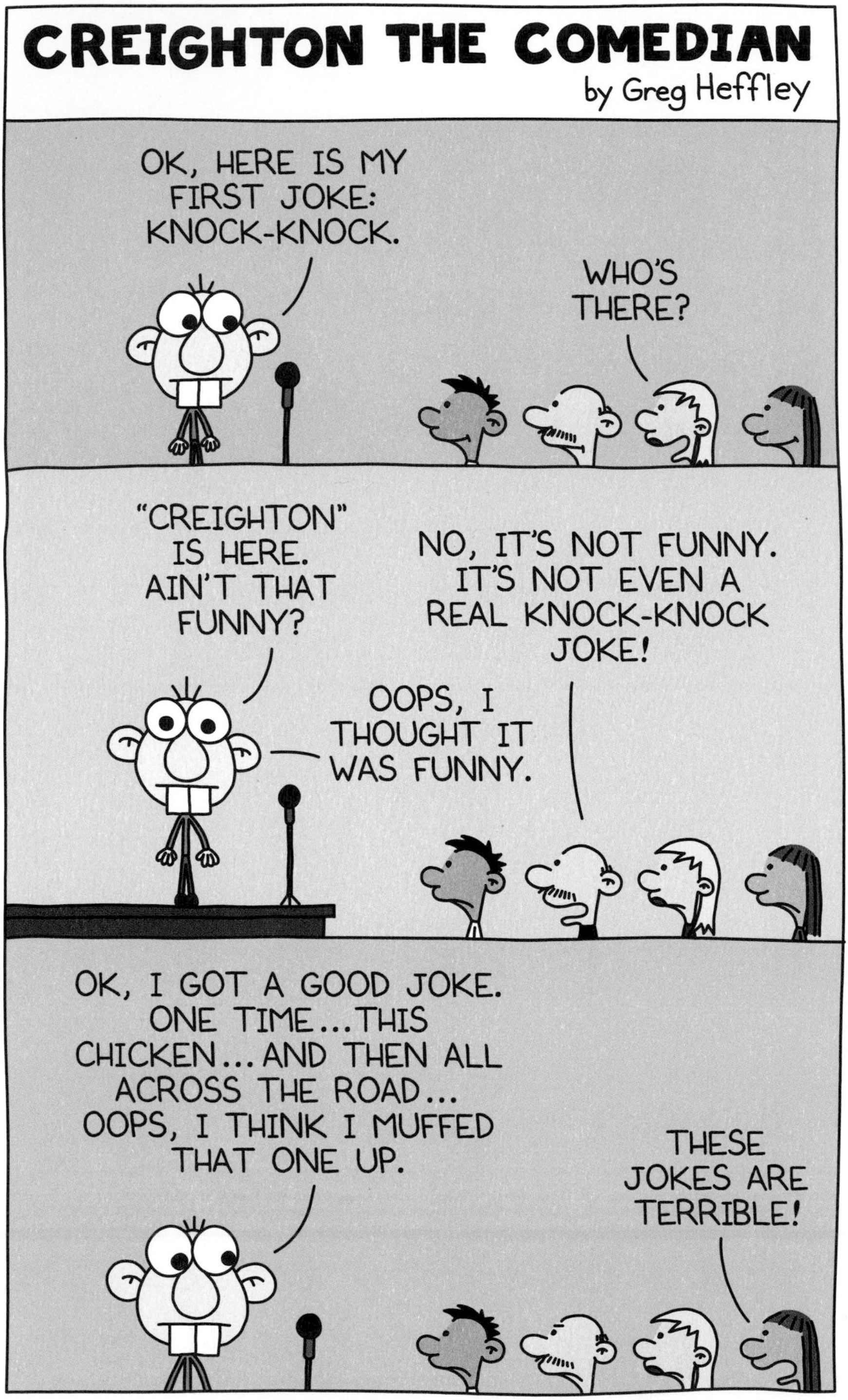
CREIGHTON THE COMEDIAN
by Greg Heffley
OK, HERE IS MY FIRST JOKE: KNOCK-KNOCK.
WHO'S THERE?
"CREIGHTON" IS HERE. AIN'T THAT FUNNY?
NO, IT'S NOT FUNNY. IT'S NOT EVEN A REAL KNOCK-KNOCK JOKE!
OOPS, I THOUGHT IT WAS FUNNY.
OK, I GOT A GOOD JOKE. ONE TIME...THIS CHICKEN...AND THEN ALL ACROSS THE ROAD... OOPS, I THINK I MUFFED THAT ONE UP.
THESE JOKES ARE TERRIBLE!

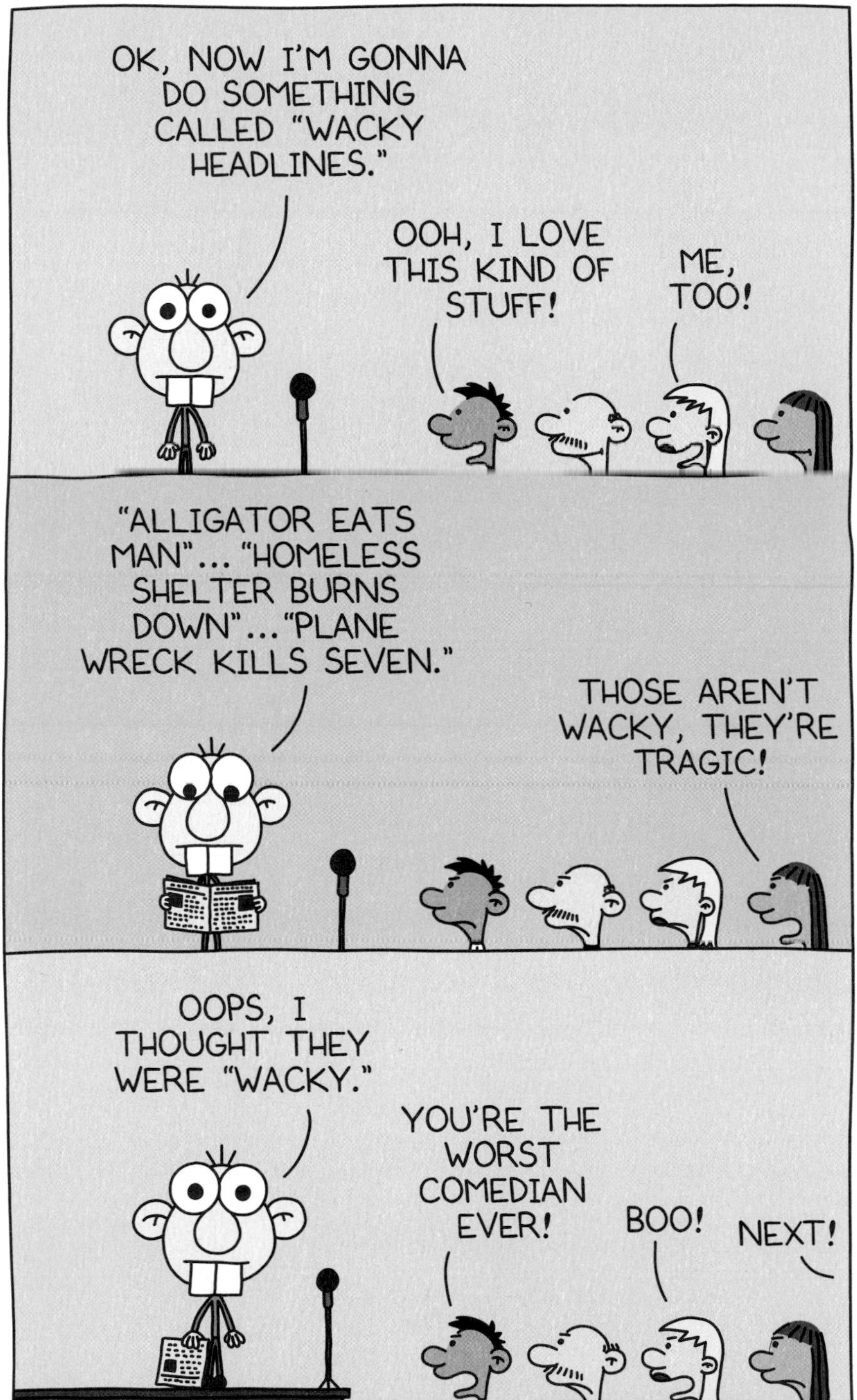
OK, NOW I'M GONNA DO SOMETHING CALLED "WACKY HEADLINES."
OOH, I LOVE THIS KIND OF STUFF!
ME, TOO!
"ALLIGATOR EATS MAN"... "HOMELESS SHELTER BURNS DOWN"... "PLANE WRECK KILLS SEVEN."
THOSE AREN'T WACKY, THEY'RE TRAGIC!
OOPS, I THOUGHT THEY WERE "WACKY."
YOU'RE THE WORST COMEDIAN EVER!
BOO!
NEXT!

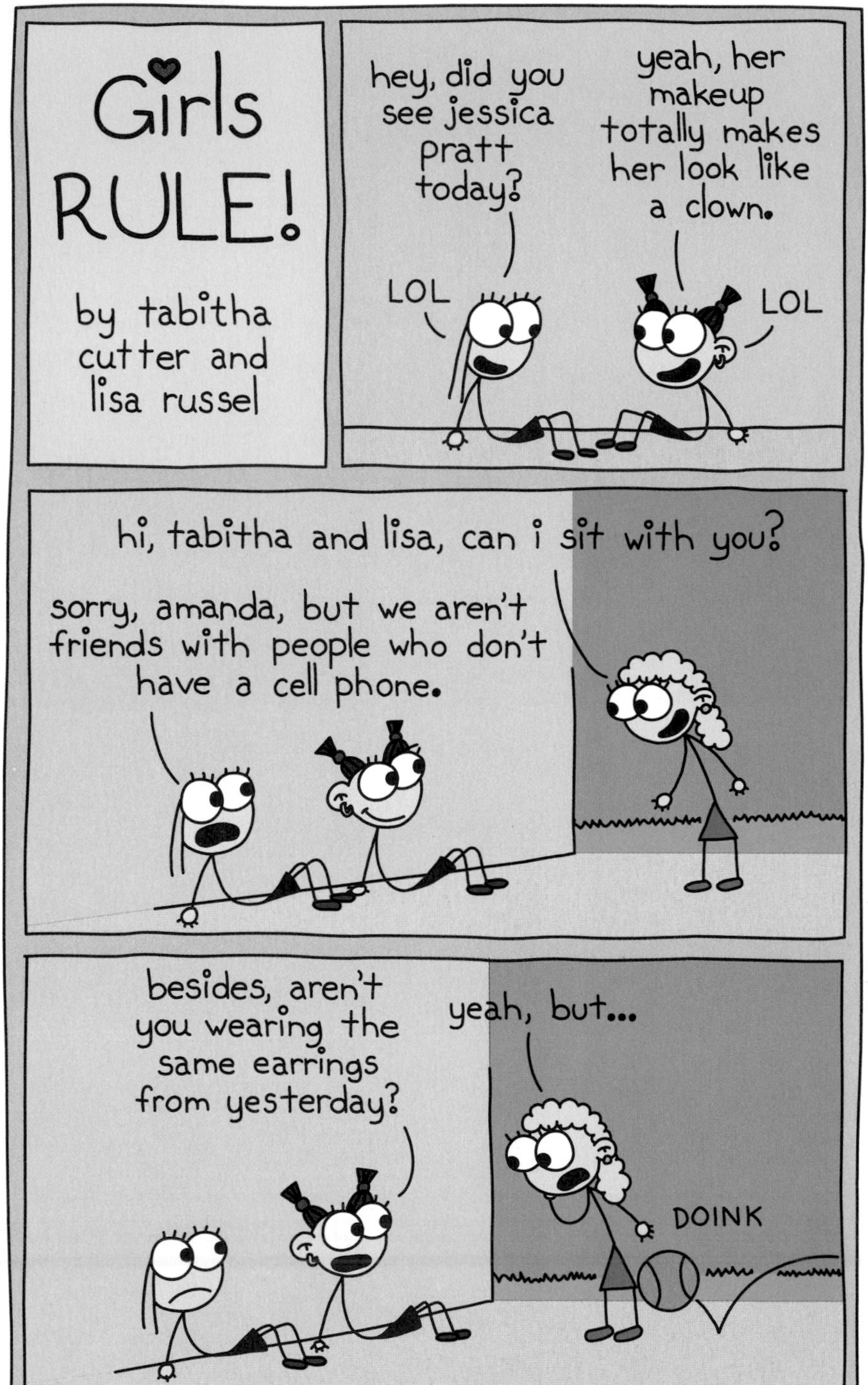
Girls RULE!
by tabitha cutter and lisa russel
hey, did you see jessica pratt today?
yeah, her makeup totally makes her look like a clown.
LOL
LOL
hi, tabitha and lisa, can i sit with you?
sorry, amanda, but we aren't friends with people who don't have a cell phone.
besides, aren't you wearing the same earrings from yesterday?
yeah, but...
DOINK

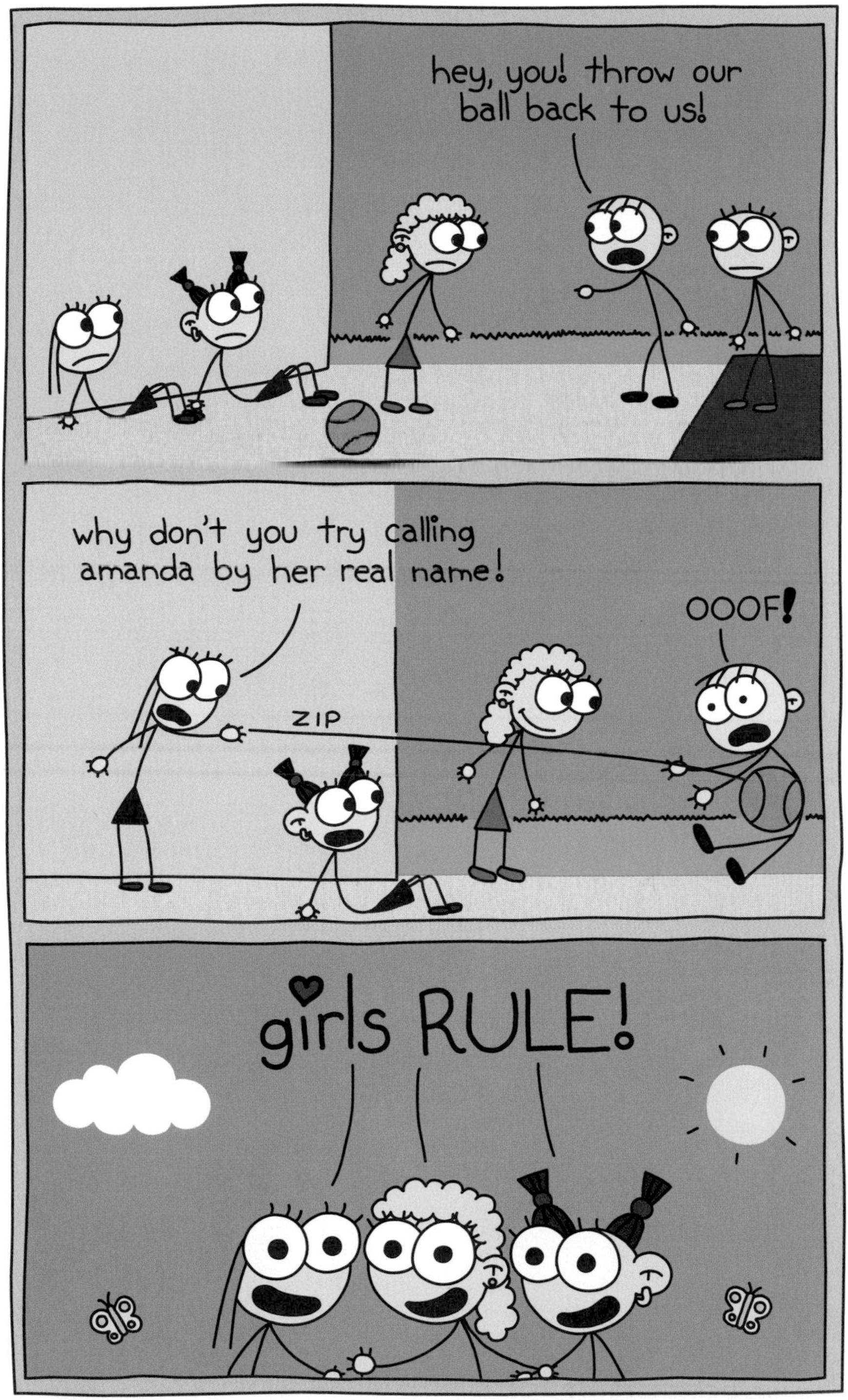
hey, you! throw our ball back to us!
why don't you try calling amanda by her real name!
ZIP
OOOF!
girls RULE!

JEROME

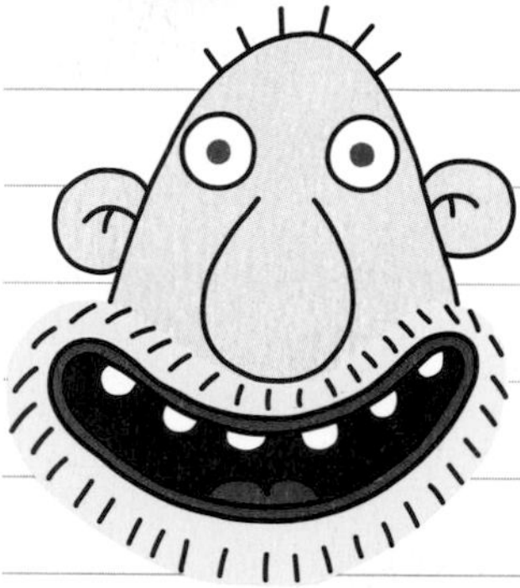

the man with **INCREDIBLY** RED LIPS

BY GREG HEFFLEY

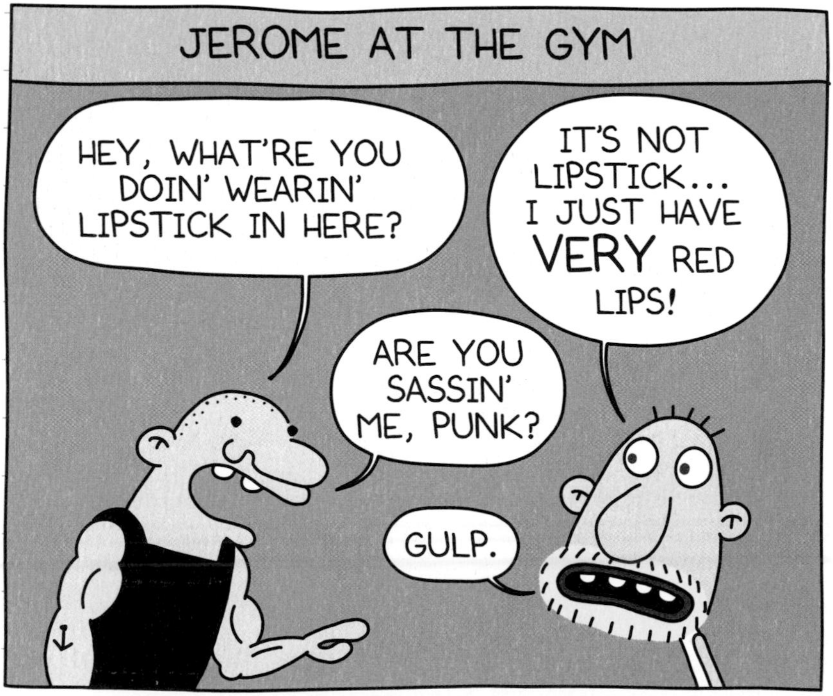

JEROME AT THE GYM
HEY, WHAT'RE YOU DOIN' WEARIN' LIPSTICK IN HERE?
IT'S NOT LIPSTICK... I JUST HAVE VERY RED LIPS!
ARE YOU SASSIN' ME, PUNK?
GULP.

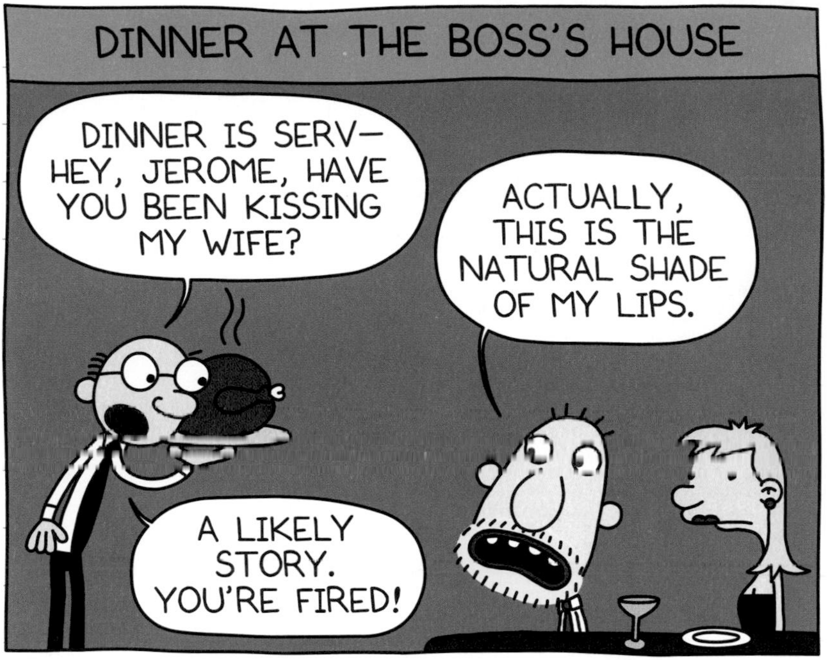
DINNER AT THE BOSS'S HOUSE
DINNER IS SERV— HEY, JEROME, HAVE YOU BEEN KISSING MY WIFE?
ACTUALLY, THIS IS THE NATURAL SHADE OF MY LIPS.
A LIKELY STORY. YOU'RE FIRED!

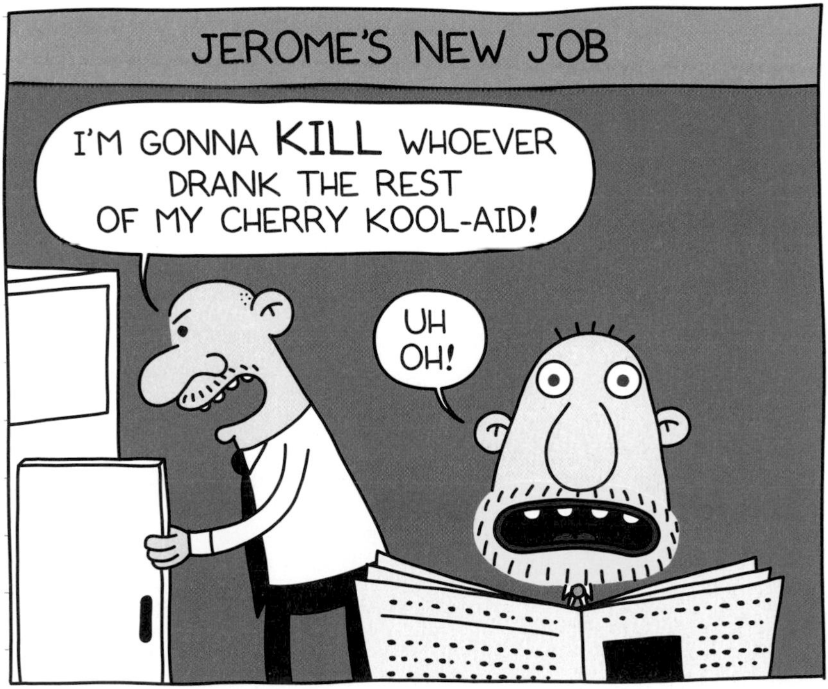
JEROME'S NEW JOB
I'M GONNA KILL WHOEVER DRANK THE REST OF MY CHERRY KOOL-AID!
UH OH!

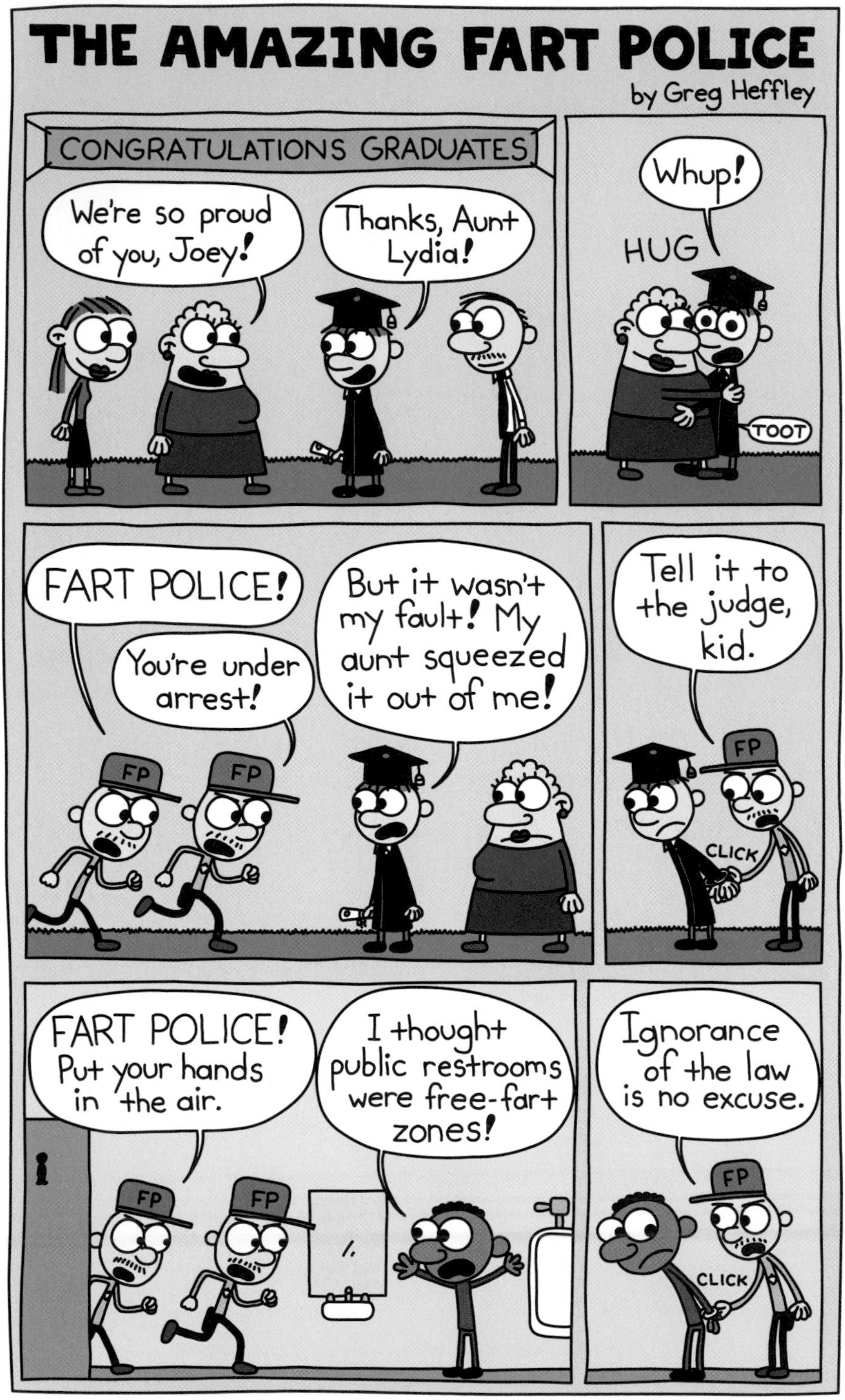
THE AMAZING FART POLICE
by Greg Heffley
CONGRATULATIONS GRADUATES
We're so proud of you, Joey!
Thanks, Aunt Lydia!
Whup!
HUG
TOOT
FART POLICE!
You're under arrest!
But it wasn't my fault! My aunt squeezed it out of me!
Tell it to the judge, kid.
CLICK
FART POLICE! Put your hands in the air.
I thought public restrooms were free-fart zones!
Ignorance of the law is no excuse.
CLICK

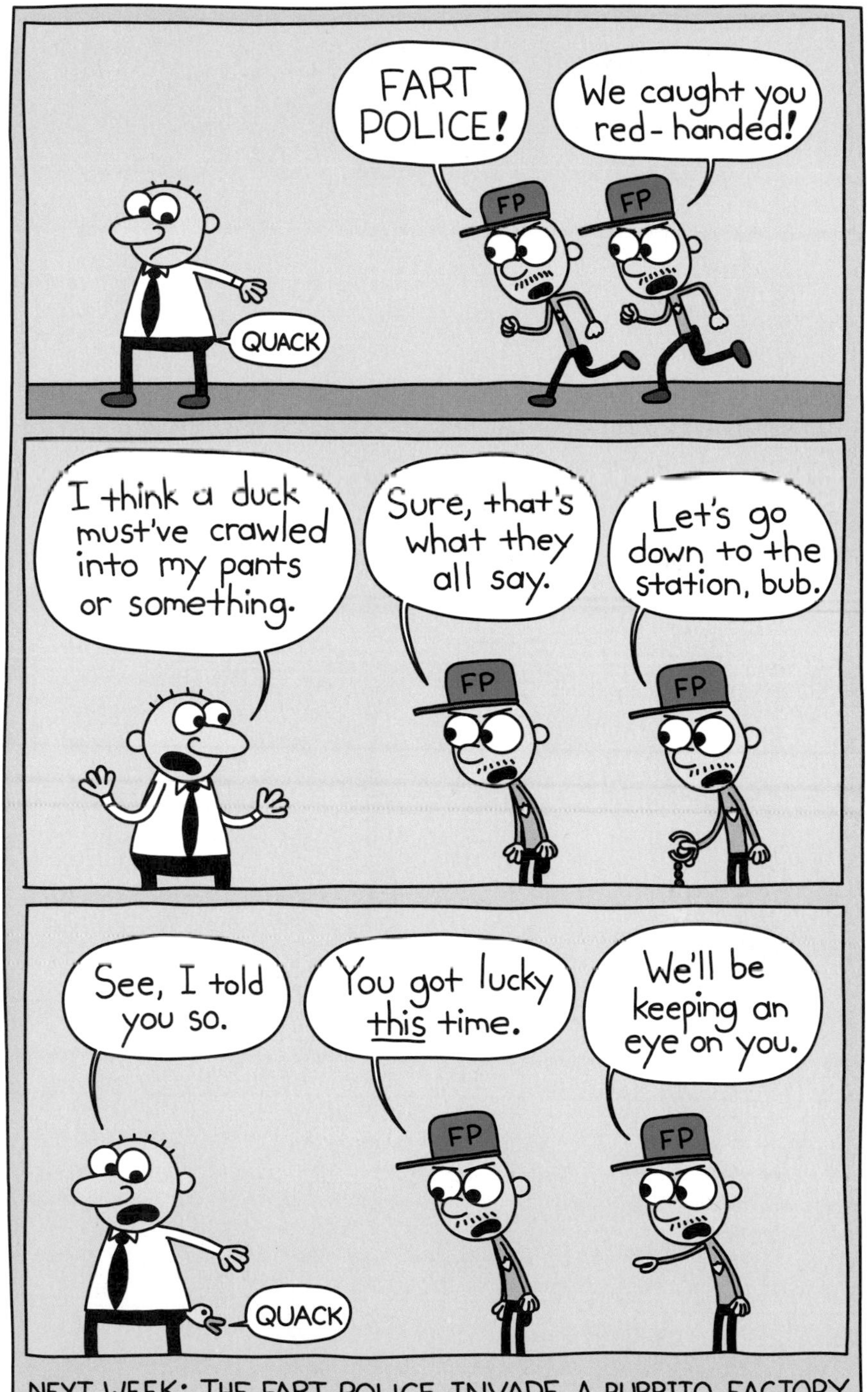
FART POLICE!
We caught you red-handed!
QUACK
I think a duck must've crawled into my pants or something.
Sure, that's what they all say.
Let's go down to the station, bub.
See, I told you so.
You got lucky this time.
We'll be keeping an eye on you.
QUACK
NEXT WEEK: THE FART POLICE INVADE A BURRITO FACTORY

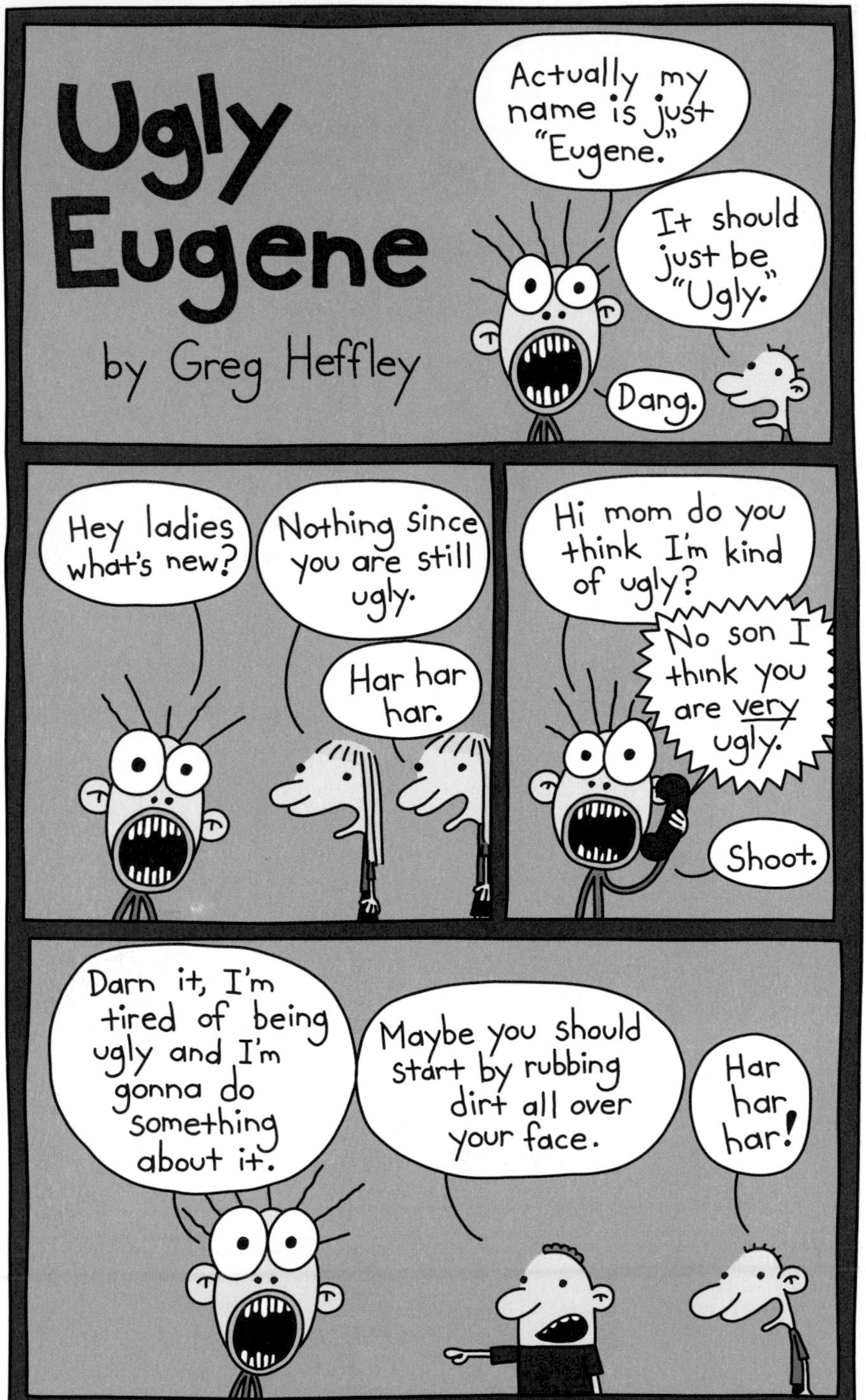
Ugly Eugene
by Greg Heffley
Actually my name is just "Eugene."
It should just be "Ugly."
Dang.
Hey ladies what's new?
Nothing since you are still ugly.
Har har har.
Hi mom do you think I'm kind of ugly?
No son I think you are very ugly.
Shoot.
Darn it, I'm tired of being ugly and I'm gonna do something about it.
Maybe you should start by rubbing dirt all over your face.
Har har har!

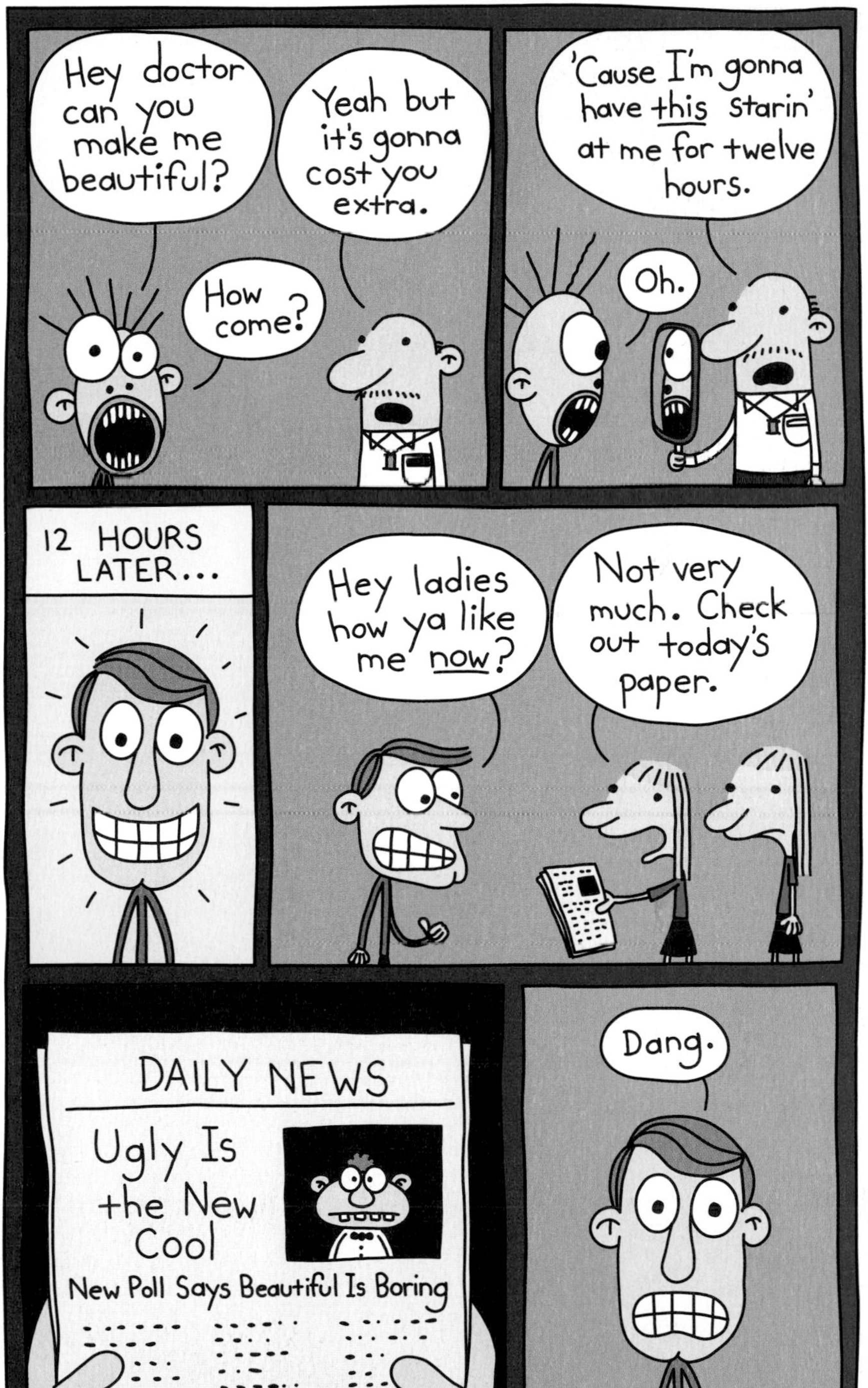
Hey doctor can you make me beautiful?
Yeah but it's gonna cost you extra.
How come?
'Cause I'm gonna have this starin' at me for twelve hours.
Oh.
12 HOURS LATER...
Hey ladies how ya like me now?
Not very much. Check out today's paper.
DAILY NEWS
Ugly Is the New Cool
New Poll Says Beautiful Is Boring
Dang.

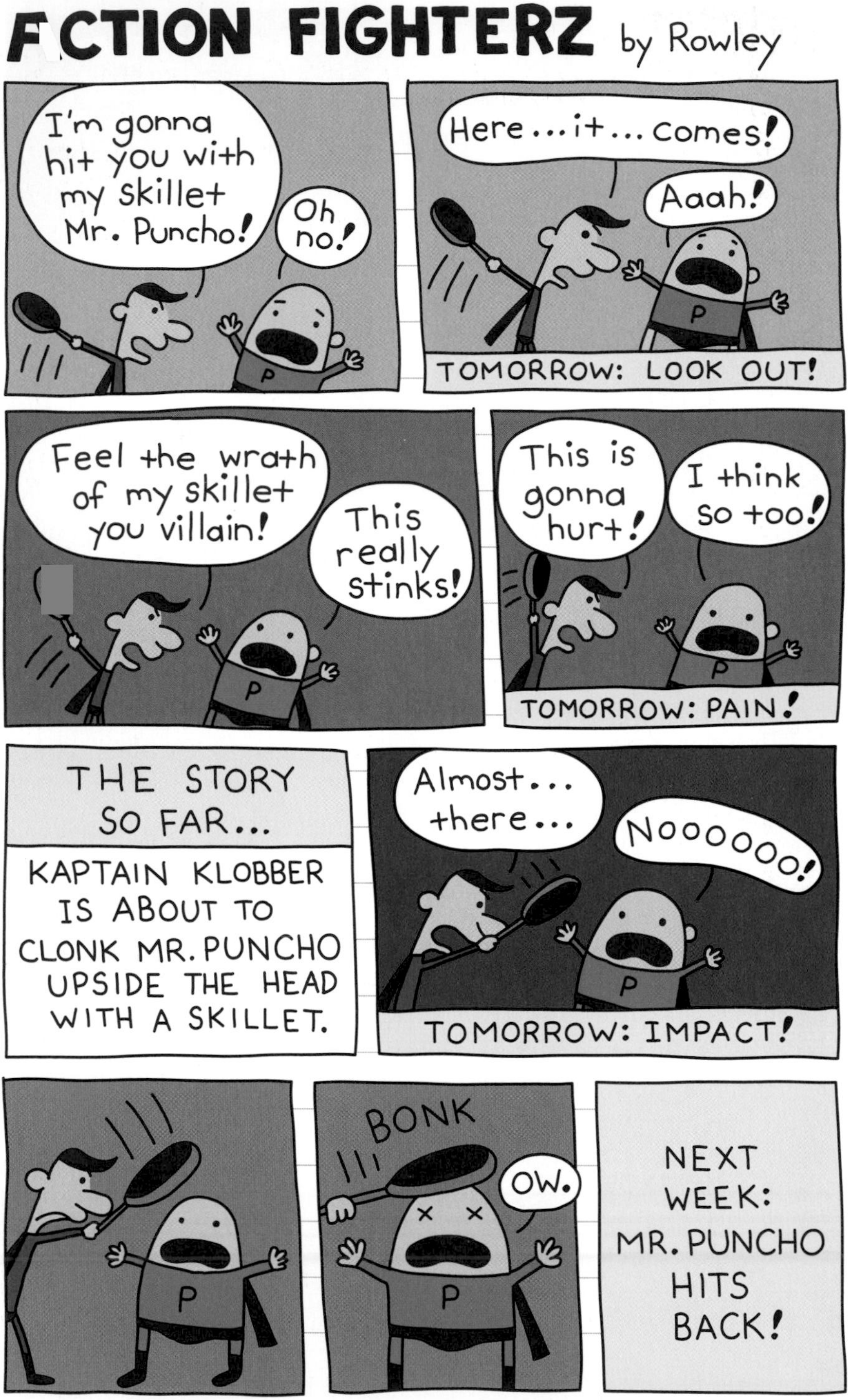
FCTION FIGHTERZ by Rowley
I'm gonna hit you with my skillet Mr. Puncho!
Oh no!
Here...it...comes!
Aaah!
TOMORROW: LOOK OUT!
Feel the wrath of my skillet you villain!
This really stinks!
This is gonna hurt!
I think so too!
TOMORROW: PAIN!
THE STORY SO FAR...
KAPTAIN KLOBBER IS ABOUT TO CLONK MR. PUNCHO UPSIDE THE HEAD WITH A SKILLET.
Almost... there...
Noooooo!
TOMORROW: IMPACT!
BONK
OW.
NEXT WEEK: MR. PUNCHO HITS BACK!

Create your own COVER

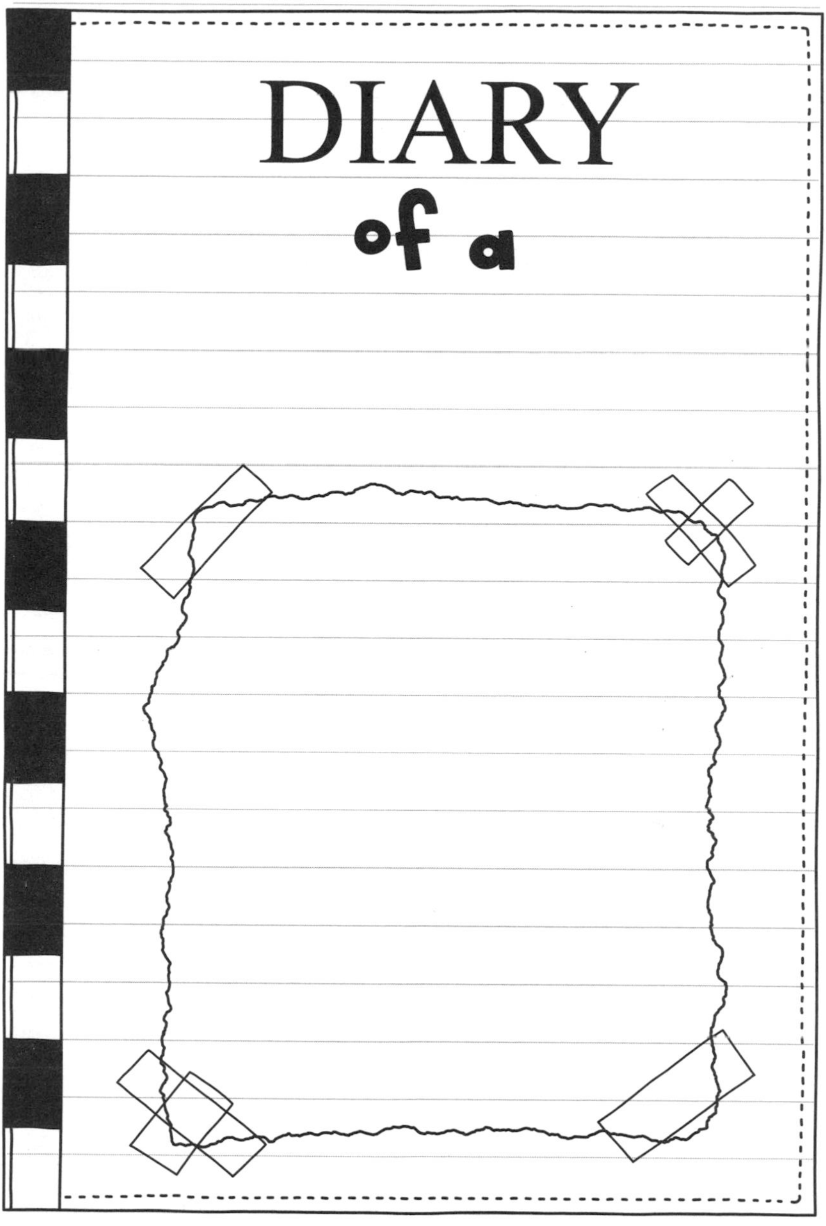
DIARY
of a

What's YOUR story?

Use the rest of this book to keep a daily journal, write a novel, draw comic strips, or tell your life story.

But whatever you do, make sure you put this book someplace safe after you finish it.

Because when you're rich and famous, this thing is gonna be worth a FORTUNE.

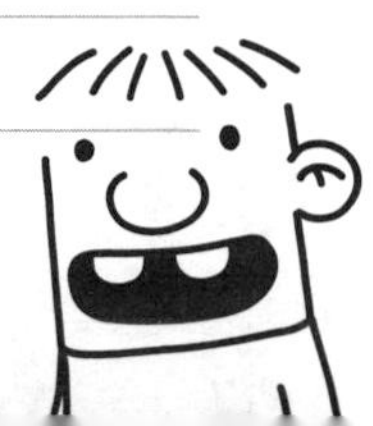

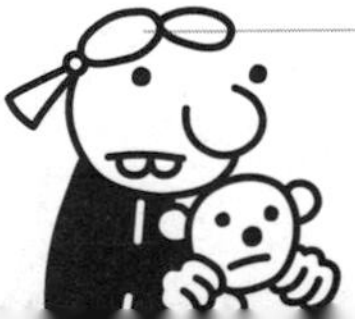

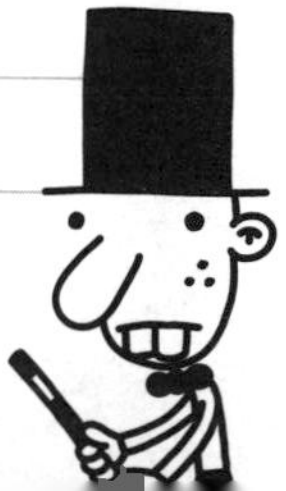

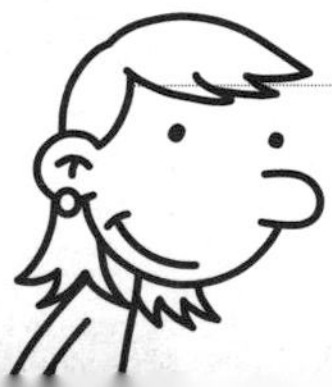

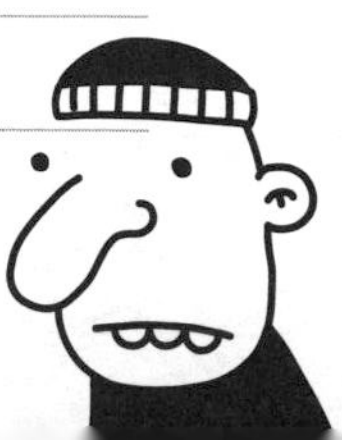

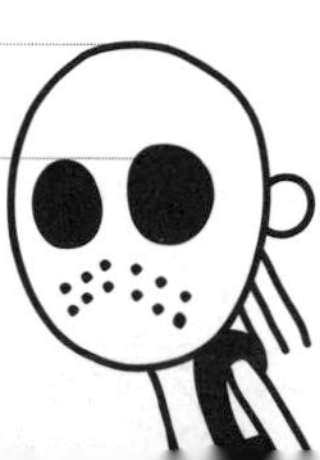

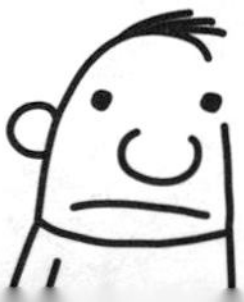

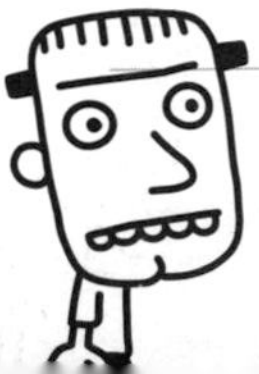

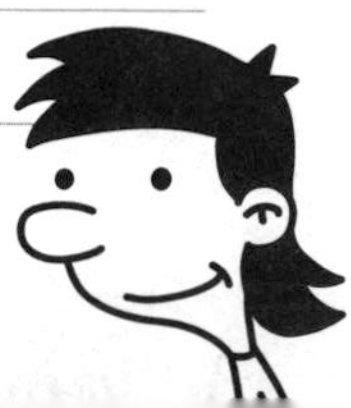

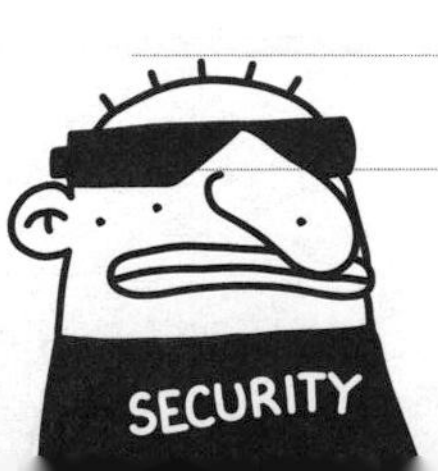
SECURITY

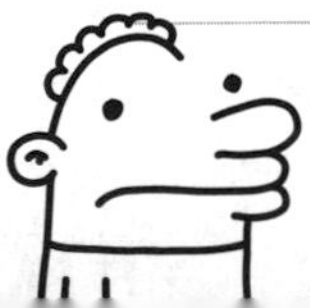

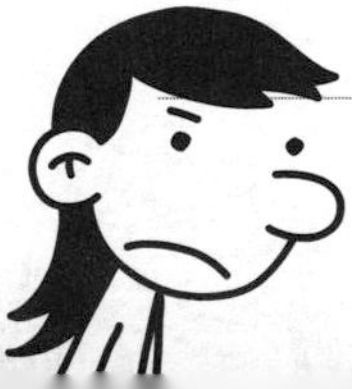

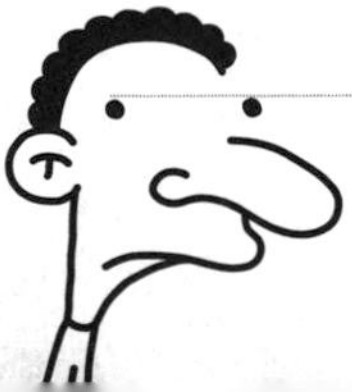

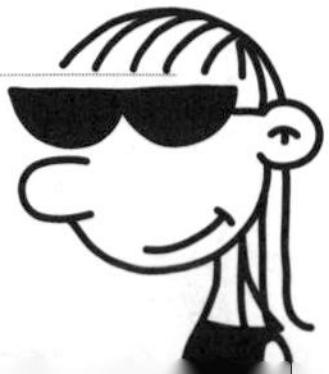

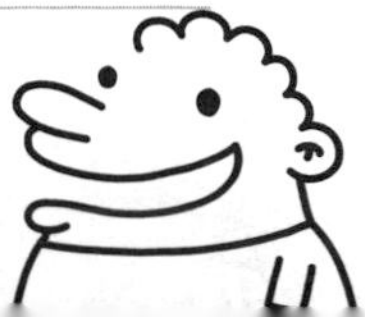

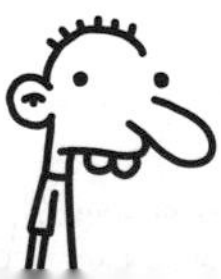

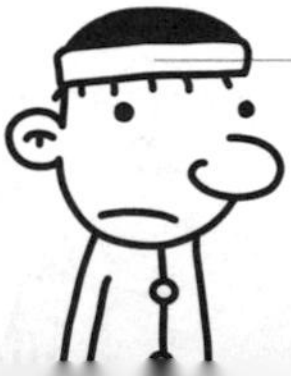

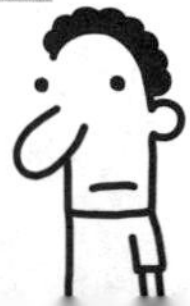

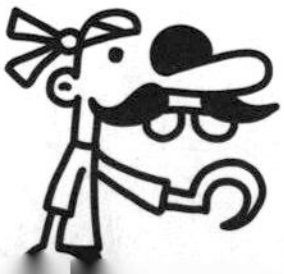

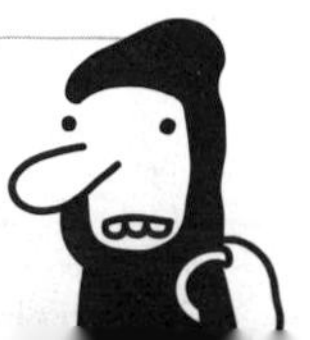

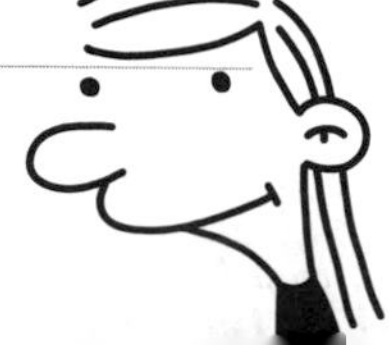

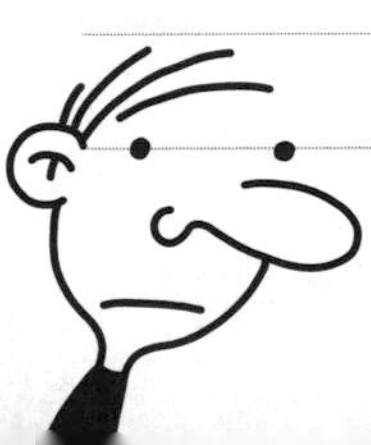

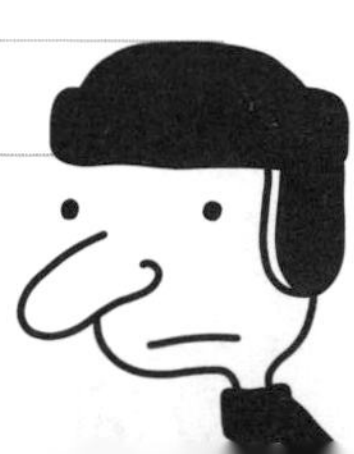

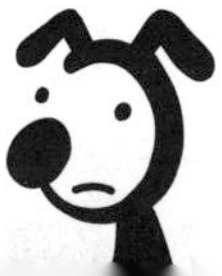

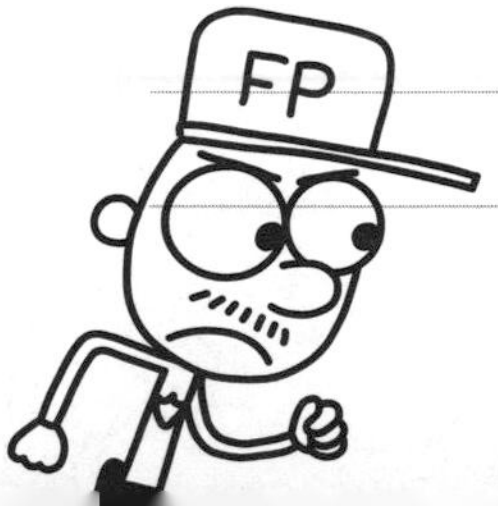
FP

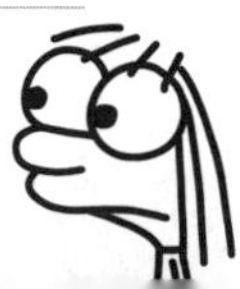

ABOUT THE AUTHOR
(THAT'S YOU)

ACKNOWLEDGMENTS
(THE PEOPLE YOU WANT TO THANK)